CRAZY LOVE

RACHAEL TAMAYO

Foster Embry Publishing, LLC
244 Fifth Avenue, Suite E148
New York, New York 10001
www.fosterembry.com

Printed in the United States of America

First edition, 2017
Second edition, 2018
Third edition, 2022

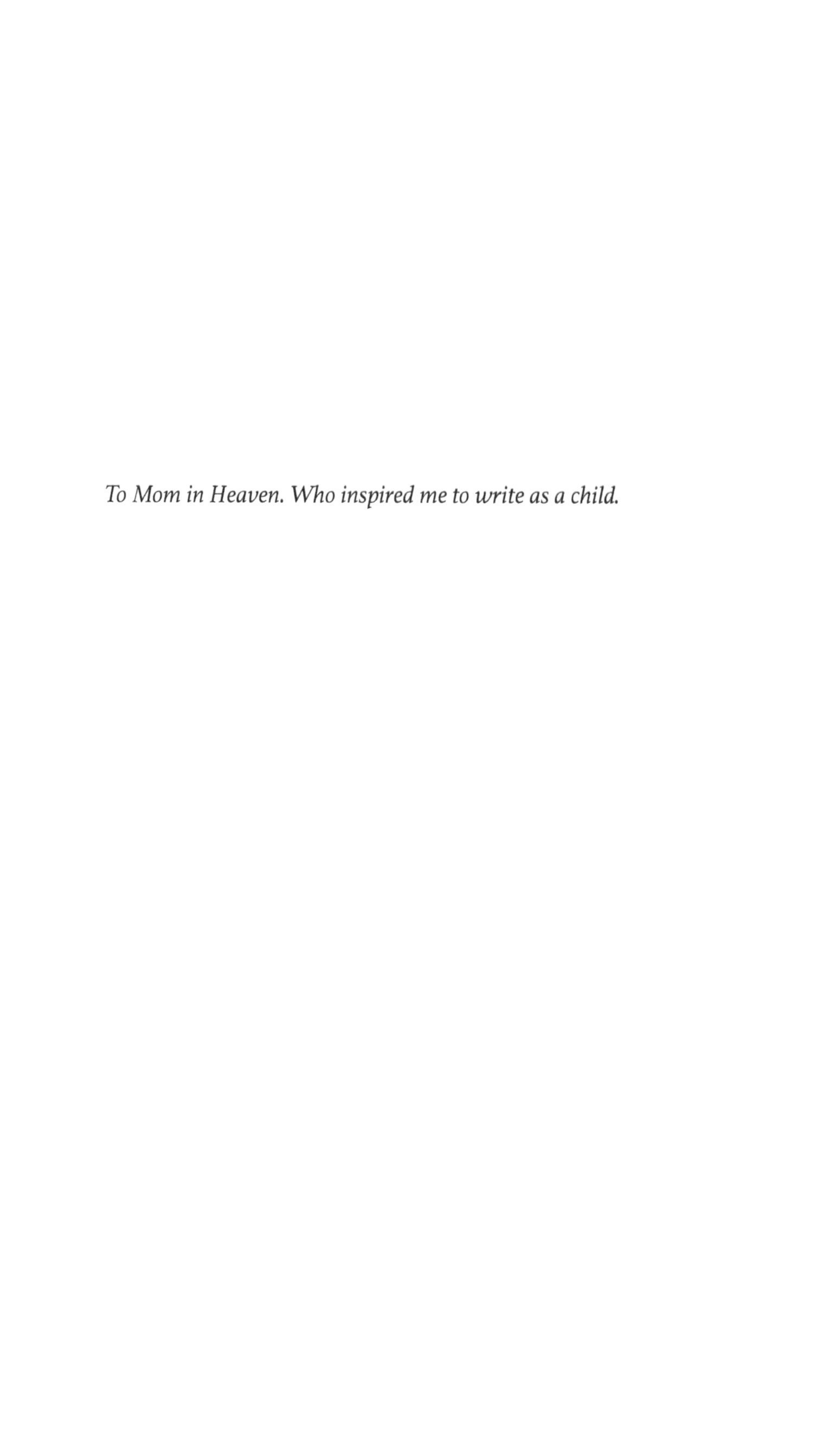

To Mom in Heaven. Who inspired me to write as a child.

CHAPTER 1

NOAH

The rain beats down on my car as I sit in the parking lot. My eyes dart from the door of the CVS to the clock in the dash. It's almost time for her to leave. Raindrops bead and drip down my windshield as I grab the oversized umbrella in the seat beside me.

A smile reaches my face as I imagine how happy she will be when she sees that I thought to meet her at the door. Water sloshes over my leather shoes and the cuffs of my suit pants are dampened as I trudge through puddles, holding the umbrella high. Under the overhang, I close the umbrella and check my phone again. She's going to be coming out any moment now. My heart rate picks up a little bit. I can almost see her bright red hair and those big, round brown eyes as she smiles up at me and hear her say my name as she greets me.

The doors open. I hold my breath, turning, hoping. It's only a little, elderly woman. She's not looking as she fishes keys out of a small purse dangling from her arm.

The doors open again. I see that bright red hair before I see anything else. Gripping the umbrella, I watch the doors open, my heart slamming against my ribs.

"Bye!" Her voice is lilting as she waves goodbye to someone in the store.

She's not carrying an umbrella. This won't do. *What if she got sick from getting wet?* I'll have to speak to her about taking better care of herself. I won't have her being careless.

"Emily, hi." I say, stepping into her path.

Those brown eyes stir up something deep inside me as she turns towards me. Emily sidesteps me. Her smile flickers a bit before resting on her lips. She takes a deep breath and glances towards her car, keys in hand.

"Hello there, Mr. Burrell. How are you today?"

"Terrible weather, isn't it? Headed home?"

"To a friend's engagement party, actually. I'm running a bit late. I got stuck on the phone. You don't like the rain?"

I shake my head. "I prefer sunshine. And I've told you before, call me Noah."

She shifts her weight, glancing at her car again. "I hate to rush off, but I have to get going. My friend will be wondering where I am. I'm sure the night pharmacist can help you."

Surely, she realizes that she's the only reason I come by every day. She's teasing me. I smile. "Let me walk you to your car. I have an umbrella."

"I'm fine. I'm not parked far. Thank you."

"I insist. I won't have you getting sick."

She blows out a breath. "It's no problem. It's not cold out. Don't trouble yourself." She starts out into the rain.

I reach out and grab her by the elbow. My hand on her skin sends heat through me. I've never touched her before this moment. Stopping, she turns back and looks at me. Pulling carefully away from my grip, she deprives me of the skin left revealed by her short-sleeved polo shirt.

"Seriously, I'm fine," she says sternly.

Normally I'd never tolerate this... attitude. This... defiance. But this is Emily. My Emily. She doesn't understand yet, but she will. Once she understands, she will thank me.

"Of course you are. But why deprive a man the chance to do a gentlemanly good deed for the day?"

Defeat fills her eyes as she nods, motioning with a gesture for me to come with her. I walk by her side, which is where I'm meant to be. She's close to me, under the protective umbrella and sheltered from the rain. I linger as she opens her car door, gets inside, sticks her keys in the ignition, and then looks up at me. "Thank you, Mr. Burrell."

"It was my pleasure, Emily. Tell Caroline good luck in her engagement for me."

I walk off, feeling her eyes on my back, realizing my mistake. Maybe it's my imagination and she didn't catch it. I hear the car door slam, and I chastise myself for the slip. I shouldn't have said Caroline's name. I walk towards the store until I know she's driven off, and then head back to my car, silently cursing myself. Damn it.

Surely Emily will understand. *Women like men that pay attention, don't they?* She will be pleased with me for watching over her. I toss the umbrella into the back seat of my car, assuring myself that my Emily knows me better than this. She won't be angry. She will be flattered.

I have just enough time to get to dinner before heading to her house. I need to give her time to leave before going in to check my cameras.

EMILY

I must have mentioned her name. I don't remember doing it, but surely I did. It's the only way he would know it. *Isn't it?*

Noah Burrell is an irritation to me and nothing more. I'd love for a day to go by without him popping up in the pharmacy window to say hello. This middle-aged guy is probably just lonely, but I don't see why. He's practically made of money and sure to tell me about his business or drop hints about his wealth at least once a week.

At first, I thought it was cute. He's an older guy just being friendly. He's handsome, in that distinguished sort of way, but I've never been one to go after older men. After awhile, I realized that he was singling me out every time he came into the store. Now it's been months and it's just getting creepy. My coworkers tease me, telling me that he's my sugar-daddy boyfriend.

I suppose that I'm too nice. I should just tell him point-blank that he's getting nowhere, but he hasn't actually done anything but be friendly. He's never asked me out. He's never touched me, until today when he grabbed me to keep me from going into the rain.

Shaking my head, I pull into my driveway. I dial Caroline's number as I get out of the car and run to the front door, dodging raindrops.

"Where are you? I thought you'd be on your way by now." She groans into the phone as soon as she picks up.

"I just got home. I was delayed at work. Come on, you know what that's like."

I bend to scratch my dog, Maxie's head as she dances all around me. My little brown and white King Charles Cavalier Spaniel wiggles her little butt and licks my hand.

"Hurry up."

"Why are you so nervous? You know all these people, don't you?" I kick off my shoes on the way across my already cluttered living room, dropping my purse in a chair.

"Most of them. Announcing an engagement is a big deal, okay? His mom already hates me. I have to make sure this is all perfect."

I laugh, kicking off my jeans. "That's what mothers-in-laws do, isn't it? She'll get over it. I have to go. I'll text you when I'm on my way." I hang up before she answers and toss my phone on the bed.

I slip into a black halter dress and heels, refresh my face, and fluff my hair. After a spritz of perfume, I toss my lipstick, wallet, and keys into my clutch.

I crouch to kiss Maxie. "See you later, Maxie. Be a good girl and guard the house." After making sure she has food and water, and that her doggy door is open, I head back out into the rain.

Caroline's fiancé's house is big. He comes from old money and is in medical school. I tease her by telling her she's found her meal ticket and she always rolls her eyes at me and tells me the money doesn't matter.

I squeeze my ten-year-old Toyota into a tight spot in a semi-circle driveway already full of cars and shut off the engine. She's intimidated by her fiancé's family, always has been. I suppose I can understand why, considering that trying to impress his mother has proven to be almost impossible so far. My heels click on the stone pavement as I walk up the stairs, approaching a set of double doors. Just as my finger touches the doorbell one of the doors flies open and I'm faced with a clearly stressed out Caroline. Despite this, she looks beautiful.

She's wearing an elegant off-white gown, and her dark hair is pulled into a perfect chignon. She's lovely.

I'm grabbed and pulled inside with a swift jerk. The home smells of jasmine and vanilla. Music is playing in the distance. The entryway is decorated with a picture of her and Gary celebrating their engagement.

"Calm down, what the hell." I laugh as I'm dragged out of the entry and toward the kitchen.

"Let's go get a drink."

"Why are you so nervous? You need to take a breath. Gary will handle his mom." I say as we enter the main room. My shoes fall silent on thick, burgundy-colored carpet.

Caroline turns to me with a deep breath. "I'm sure you're right. Gary told me the same thing. I'm just glad you're here now."

Scanning the room, I take in the people, most of whom I've never seen before, and others I've met once or twice over the two years I've known Caroline.

That's when I see him. Without a doubt, I know him. Holding a beer and smiling, he's laughing at Gary. Isaiah. I'd never forget that face or that head of blond hair.

My heart beats in my chest like a kick drum. My palms sweat.

The guy I ran from. After the hottest night I've ever shared with a man, I freaked out and ran. And here he is, not more than six feet away from me.

"Caroline, how do you know him?" I hiss, pulling her close.

"Who?"

"The blond with Gary."

She gives me a puzzled look. "He's a friend of Gary's. Why? How do you know him?"

I look up at her to see suspicion in her eyes. Okay, I admit, I never told her. I never told anyone. It just happened so fast, and then I let it all fade into the background.

EIGHT MONTHS PRIOR

A frazzled clerk at the coffee shop across from my CVS shoves a scalding hot cup of Chai tea at me. One sip tells me that it's wrong. I try to catch her attention. As I wave vigorously at her, I back into a wall of a body.

"Shit." I hear a masculine mumble.

Spinning, I see a broad chest covered by a crisp white shirt with a nice, brown stain down the front. He holds his shirt away from his skin. "God that's hot."

My face heats up. "Oh my God, I'm so sorry. Are you burned?" Placing my cup on the closest table, I grab a handful of napkins and start blotting at his shirt.

His blond head pops up. I'm met with copper eyes and a chiseled jawline, and then a smile. Uh-oh. I have a terrible weakness for cute, blond men. And damn, is he cute. Even covered in steaming hot liquid, he's adorable.

"I think I'm fine." He meets my eyes.

"Let me buy you another coffee, and maybe a shirt?" I sigh, tossing the coffee stained napkins in the nearest trash can.

He glances down at his shirt again, laughing lightly. "I have another one in my office, I think. I keep a spare, in case of clumsy, cute redheads."

I flush and grin at him. Tucking a lock of my fiery hair behind my ear, I continue. "What did you order? I'll get you another one. Can you wait? Are you in a hurry?"

He glances at his watch. "No, I can wait. It's no problem, it was an accident. What's your name?"

"Emily Bronte." I stick out my hand.

"Isaiah Penrose." He takes my hand, which is swallowed in his grip. Heat travels up my arm and makes my stomach flip inside me.

I'm in deep trouble. His smile, ugh. He even has a dimple. I'm an hour late to work, thanks to cutie pie. I totally lost track of time while having coffee with him. We exchanged phone numbers.

Two hours later, I'm lost in the world of reading unreadable doctors' prescriptions when my cell phone rings.

"Hello." I snap without looking at who it is.

"Is this the number that I call to report a second-degree burn?" I hear laughter in the man's voice.

My mood instantly changes. "Hi. You didn't waste any time, did you?"

"I have tickets to tomorrow night's Clint Black concert. I was thinking maybe we could meet up and spend the day at the rodeo carnival?"

I tap my pen on the desk. "It's been ages since I've been to the rodeo."

"Is that a yes?"

I smile. "Yes, definitely. What time?"

"Um, how's noon? Can I pick you up?"

I rattle off my address. Normally, I would hesitate to let a stranger pick me up, but he's a cop, a detective with the Katy Police Department. Katy is a small city just outside of Houston, Texas, which I call home. I work in Katy, but live in Houston, as many that live here do.

The next day with him turns out to be the best date I've ever had. All day at the carnival eating greasy food and playing games. It's like something out of a movie. I'm weighed down with stuffed animals by the time the concert starts, and he's laughing at me as I shove a pile of teddy bears in his lap so I can stand up and scream when Clint Black comes on stage.

An hour later, I'm feeling all warm and fuzzy inside when he moves behind me, sliding his arms around my waist. His body flush against mine, his lips against my ear. A chill rolls down my spine. We've been laughing and talking all day long. I've never connected with anyone so fast in my life, which scares me. Not enough to stop what I know is coming though.

He hasn't kissed me yet. Hoping to tempt him, I turn my head and find him so close to my face that my breath catches for a second. His eyes glitter in the flashing lights, a slow country song in the air. Instead of waiting, I turn, facing him.

He's tall, but not so tall that I can't reach up and kiss him if I want to. His full lips are shaped in a perfect inviting curve. They look so soft. I reach up and touch his chest. He's wearing a Clint Black t-shirt that clings to his bulging biceps and broad, hard chest. His light wash jeans hang loose, but tight enough to see that he has a nice behind, one I'm hoping to get my hands on.

I meet his light-colored eyes, hoping that he will take the hint. I take a step into him. I'm all but flush against his body now. Something in my chest hitches when he lowers his head. He smells like Hugo cologne and his lips are even softer than they look. As soon as our lips collide, we both combust. He grabs my face in both hands, stealing my breath as his mouth opens and our tongues tangle together. I whimper in delight, curling my arms around his neck, pulling him against my chest.

Isaiah nibbles on my lips as his hands drift down my back to my ass. His hands are large, gently squeezing me, sliding as far down my thighs as his arms can reach before returning to my butt.

"You want to get out of here?" His voice is a whisper against my ear.

I nod. "Yes, let's go."

Forty-five minutes later I'm pinned against the front door of his apartment. The keys are in his hand, but he won't stop kissing me long enough to unlock the door. Hands planted firmly by my head, keys dangling off his finger, his mouth devours mine. I grab him by his belt and pull his hips into me.

He's breathing heavy when he finally pulls his mouth away, jabs the key in the lock, and pushes the door open. It's closed with a kick. The keys drop to the floor, as does my purse. I jump on him and he catches me as if I don't weigh a thing, holding me up as he walks us both down a hall and kicks a door open.

I'm mildly aware of being in a bedroom, but only because I'm dropped onto a queen size bed that's not made. A white down comforter is bunched up on one side, but all I can see is him.

He kneels in front of me as he pulls his shirt off. I sit up, reaching for his belt as he starts to work on the buttons of my pink and black plaid cowboy cut top, flying through them and pushing it off my shoulders.

I unbuckle his belt, glancing up at his smiling face. His jeans come open easily. I slide the zipper down, and he pushes me backwards playfully, still kneeling with open pants hanging off his hips. He stands up, and meeting my eyes, grabs my boots one at a time, pulling them off while toeing off his own boots.

I'm panting when he moves to my belt. He opens my pants with flying fingers and jerks my tight jeans down and off my legs so that I'm laying here in only black thong panties and a bra. Before he climbs on top of me, he pushes his pants off, and then straddles me in just his boxer briefs.

For a moment, I just take him in. His hair is a tousled mess from my hands being in it, and his eyes are bright. His muscled chest is heaving as he stares down at me. I graze my fingers over his abs. His muscles clench under my hand as our eyes meet. There is something different about him, about this. I can see that he's feeling it too. This doesn't feel like a one-night stand. It feels like the beginning of something.

I don't want to think about that now. It's too much, too fast. I look up into his face and his eyes catch mine as he lowers down to all fours, hovering over me. He looks softly into my face, causing my heart to stop and my insides to liquefy.

This is like nothing that's ever happened to me before.

"You are gorgeous," he says, quietly, his eyes never leaving mine.

I don't answer. Instead, I reach back and unhook my bra, freeing my breasts. His gaze is instantly pulled down. He sucks in a breath and then lowers his mouth to my body.

Gasping, we fall apart in the bed. The heat in here is unbelievable considering that only thirty minutes ago it was perfectly comfortable.

Turning my head, I see that his chest if heaving and he's got his hands over his face. I poke him in the ribs. "You okay?" I force my breathing to slow.

He uncovers his eyes and smiles. "Hell yeah, I'm way better than okay."

"Just checking. You look ready to have a heart attack or something." I tease.

He laughs. "I think I almost did."

Our eyes meet as he calms his breathing. My instinct is to get up, clean off, and call a cab. I shouldn't stay. Problem is, I'm not ready to say bye just yet.

The next morning, I wake up tangled in his blankets. Heat radiates off his body as the realization of last night hits me. The best sex of my life, all three times.

Panic clenches around my heart like a cold fist. He's going to want more from me. I could see it in his eyes last night. I felt it in his touch. Carefully, I get out of bed and start the search for my clothes. They are scattered all over a cluttered bedroom. Isaiah snores lightly in the bed, never stirring.

I like him. I like him a lot and that's what scares me. I don't even know why it does, but I'm terrified.

I slip out of his room, dressing quickly. I retrieve my phone from my purse and Google the number for a cab company.

Glancing around the room, a twinge of guilt hits me. Regret. Something screaming in my brain telling me I'm a fool, just calm down and don't panic.

I take in the nice apartment for the first time. Last night I was lost in a fit of passion. We could have been in a cave and I wouldn't have noticed. One of the living room walls is all glass, a giant window in a high-rise apartment. A view of the forest, green trees. It's lovely. The couch and recliner are both gray microfiber, there is a big screen TV, and dark wooden accent tables. A small kitchen, pretty clean accept for a few dishes in the sink.

With my shoes in my hand, I slip out the front door. I really wish I had thought to grab those bears, which are locked in his car. I would've liked to keep one. God knows I'll never forget him, or last night.

Caroline snaps her fingers in my face, bringing me back from the memory. Isaiah called me a few times, but I never answered him. Didn't take him long to stop. I still regret it. By the time I realized what I did, a month had passed by and I knew that it was too late to call him.

"Sorry, what did you say?" I blink at her, looking back over at him.

"I said, how do you know him?"

I take in a deep breath, but before I can pull her away and tell her the story, he turns and sees me.

CHAPTER 2

ISAIAH

I remember that voice. It takes me back eight months to that damn rodeo date that I fooled myself into thinking was more.

I guess it was more for me than it was for her.

Turning my head, I laugh out loud at the sight of that bright, red hair. Her back is to me, but I still know it's her.

I suppose I should be annoyed or pissed off. What's the point though? It's been forever. Months. So what if I've thought about her for way too long, or that I kept hoping she might call me for weeks? I sure won't chase someone that made it abundantly clear she didn't want more from me.

But here she is. Her shoulders are bare and creamy in a black halter dress. She peeks over her shoulder. Our eyes meet across the space. She bites her lip, and I grin, laughing again as her cheeks grow crimson.

After excusing myself, I make my way over. I don't want to be the asshole that didn't say hello. "Hey there, stranger." I smile.

Caroline gives me a confused look. Emily turns and breathes deeply, looking up into my eyes.

"Hi Isaiah, small world I guess, huh?"

"Sure is. I didn't know you knew these two. How have you been?"

Emily glances between Caroline and myself. “Caroline, Isaiah and I dated a few months ago for a short while.”

Dated. I guess you could call it that.

Caroline smiles as understanding fills her eyes.

“I’ve been good, you know. Just working and stuff.” Emily looks back at me.

“I’m going to go check on the food. I’ll find you later.” Caroline smiles and walks off.

“Same here. So, burned anyone else with coffee lately?”

A slow smile creeps onto her face. I see the ice starting to thaw, the embarrassment fading away from her big brown eyes.

“Trust you to bring that up. No, just you.”

I grin. “Nice to see that smile.”

I know, I shouldn’t flirt with her. That smile, however, does the same thing to me now that it did the first time I saw it. She touches her straight hair, which falls into her face until she tucks the stray strands away. It’s longer now and cut in layers that hang a few inches past her shoulders.

She is as beautiful as ever.

“So, how do you know these two?”

“I went to school with Gary. We have one of those on again off again friendships. We stop talking for a while, and then one of us calls the other out of the blue and we start hanging out again.”

She nods, glancing down at the beer in my hand.

“You want one?” I move to go grab her one out of the tub of ice not far from where we are standing.

“Sure. Thanks.”

She sits down on the couch, wrapping a napkin around the dripping bottle. She lifts her eyes and our gaze meets, and a flash of her in my bed blinds me for a moment. I can almost hear her panting, the soft moans that made me crazy that night.

I’d love to know why she never answered the phone, but I’ll be damned if I’ll ever ask her.

An awkward silence falls between us. All I can think about is the way we crashed into my apartment, and the feeling of waking up alone, no note, no call. Nothing.

First time I ever felt used by a woman.

I sit down beside her, wondering if either of us will ever bring it up. Will we sit here and make small talk, as if it never happened, and then say a casual goodbye in a couple of hours, leaving me with even more questions than I had before?

She glances over at me more than once, takes a couple of sips of beer. I hear an intake of breath.

"Um, Isaiah, I think I owe you an apology."

You think so? "Don't worry about it, Emily."

She shakes her head. "I'm sorry, I was a jerk. I wanted to call later, but it was too late. I shouldn't have done that."

What the hell do I say to this? Yeah, you were a jerk. I thought about you every day for weeks. I still have those freaking teddy bears in my closet that you left behind. I don't really know why it bothers me. It's not like I've never had a one-night stand before. I guess I thought it was more. What a brutal way to find out you're wrong.

"Emily—"

"Isaiah," she shifts, turning to me, "I mean it. I felt bad, and I still do. I never do stuff like that. The whole thing was..." She pauses, biting her lip and picking at the label on her beer.

"It is what it is. No point in worrying about it now. Let's just forget it."

She looks at me funny. "You want to forget it?"

I flash a smile. "I mean the way you bailed. Why, you don't want me to forget something?"

She flushes. Her creamy skin blooms pink as she casts her eyes out into the room, over the people milling about in this big, expensive house.

"Well... I... I mean..." She stammers and then stands. "I'm going to go check on Caroline. I'll talk to you later, okay?"

I grin. "Okay."

I watch her walk off, and then peek over her shoulder as she enters the kitchen.

NOAH

I cruise Emily's street, looking around, checking out the front of the house. Her car isn't in the driveway. She's gone.

Pulling my black Corvette around, I park on the next street. I never park in the same place twice. Neighbors are nosey, and I don't like people in my business.

Emily is always my business.

As I park, I pull out my phone and type out a text. *Let me know if she leaves.* I hit send and slide my phone back into my pocket. It buzzes again just as Emily's back fence comes into view.

Will do. She's here now.

Satisfied that I'm safe, for now, I walk around to the gate. My heart starts to beat out an abnormal rhythm in my chest, anticipating everything that is my Emily—her scent, her bed, all the things that she touches every day. My mouth starts to water as I put my hand on the gate latch.

Entering the unlocked gate that leads to her back yard, I cross on swift legs to the back door. As always, I find the spare key hidden in the potted palm by the back door. Her little dog Maxie barks through the door until I get it open and then greets me with a wiggle and furiously wagging tail. The first few times I came I brought her treats, now she follows me around like she's my dog too. Of course, soon she will be.

I can't stand clutter and it's the first thing that I see when I walk in. Everywhere. The kitchen is dirty; there are dishes piled up in the sink and an overflowing trash can. The living room isn't any better; there are clothes on the floor and a collection of coffee cups on the table.

I take a deep breath. She needs to be taught, that's all. She's smart, my girl Emily. Once she knows the rules, she'll be grateful for them. Until then, I swallow down the urge to toss the dirty dishes on the floor and walk past them. That's not why I'm here.

My loafers click on light-colored, hardwood floors as I pass through the front of the house and down the hall to her bedroom.

Her dog is still on my heels when I push the door to her bedroom open. Once again, I am assaulted by the clutter. Her bed is unmade and the covers are on the floor in a tangled swirl. It's a nice bed too—padded, grey, tufted headboard with pine furniture.

I approach the bed, cracking my knuckles to stop myself from making it. Leaning over, I pick up her pillow and bury my face in it. I breathe in the scent of her perfume and shampoo. It calms something deep inside me.

Circling around the bed, I kick laundry out of the way. I'll hire a maid for her when we are finally together. She clearly needs me.

Opening her top drawer, I pick up a pair of her silk thong panties and finger the fabric. Touching lingerie that's been close to her skin makes me breathe hard. One day, she will lay in this bed and look at me with those big brown eyes and beg me to take these panties off of her. She'll arch as I slip my fingers over her body, into her, and she will know how deep our love really is.

She needs time to understand her true feelings. When she sees how I take care of her, she won't ever want to leave. Not that I'd ever let that happen, of course.

I pocket the panties, and I move out of the bedroom to the living room where her laptop sits. It took me two weeks, but I finally figured out her password. She's too smart to use the common stuff. I knew she would be. She likes to challenge me. It's why she makes me wait to be with her. I type it in and the laptop comes to life.

I open her internet and browse her history. Nothing special, mostly bills and Amazon, books specifically. I take a moment to overlook her book selections before I head back to a site that caught my attention. I find her student loan and use the saved password to log in. She still owes fifteen thousand. I pull out my credit card and pay the bill for her with a few clicks. This will be a nice surprise for her when she goes to make her next payment. I can't wait to see her face.

I love sitting here, feeling close to her. It's getting late though and tonight I can't hide in the attic like I do sometimes and watch her. I have a very early meeting and I know if I stay, I won't be able to leave her.

As I set the computer back where I found it, I check my watch for the time. She will probably be home soon. I need to get out of here. After one last pass through her bedroom, I grab her t-shirt off the floor and inhale the scent of her body one more time. I only take her clothes when I'm really missing her. It seems that the more time goes by, the further under my skin she seems to burrow.

It's okay, her smile tells me that she feels it too. We will be together soon. Timing is everything. My Emily knows this. We are so in sync. She's waiting for the right moment to tell me to come for her.

CHAPTER 3

EMILY

I find Caroline in the kitchen getting chewed out by her future mother-in-law for using "cheap plastic plates" for the food. I clear my throat, effectively making my presence known. Her mother-in-law sighs, tosses the plastic plate aside, and walks out of the kitchen.

"You okay?" I ask.

Caroline nods. "Fine. She's such a snob. Thinks I should use real plates. It's not that formal of a party. She'll get over it." She waves a hand towards the door. "Tell me about what happened out there."

I sigh, taking a drink of my beer. "One-night stand. That's what happened. We connected, *really* connected, and I flipped out and ran before he woke up."

Might as well be honest.

She snickers. "No kidding? He's so cute, too. You and him? I had no idea. Why did you freak out?"

"I don't know why I freaked out. I regretted it later, but it was too late. We clicked, big time. It was on a whole different level. I've never had that before. I guess I panicked." I shrug.

"So, what about now?"

I smile down at my beer bottle. "Yeah right. Like he'd trust me now. I did tell him I'm sorry."

"Just now?"

"Yeah. He acted like it was no big deal. It's been a while. I guess by now it's not."

She shoves me lightly. "So go talk to him. Maybe you two can rekindle the flame."

"Whatever. I'm sure it's too late for that. He is still so damn cute, though."

She laughs, shoving me again. "Go, talk to him. You never know."

With an eye roll, I walk out of the kitchen and leave her alone with her plastic plates.

I bide my time for a while. Later, I find him sitting with someone I don't recognize. I was going to approach him, but get cold feet at the last minute and pass him as I head for the back patio, making accidental eye contact when he looks up at me.

"Hey there." I hear his deep voice behind me moments later and it makes me smile.

Turning, I lean on the railing. *What might have happened if I hadn't left? If I'd stayed that morning and lingered to look into this face in the morning light of his bedroom?* These pretty eyes that are looking down on me with mild amusement and curiosity as he stands in front of me.

"Hi."

His chuckle fills the air around us, making me smile. It lightens the awkwardness of the mood between us.

"So, what do you say we just kind of... start over?" He cocks an eyebrow at me.

Start over? What's that mean? Pretend it didn't happen? Be friends?

"Sure, why not. It was a while ago. I really am sorry though." I wince.

"You could've called. I would've answered."

"Weren't you mad?" I look up.

He meets my eyes, giving me a slight shiver.

"No, not really mad. Just disappointed."

He's still looking me in the eyes and it feels like he's pulling me in.

Right back to where I was that night, the itch to be close to him starting to bubble up.

Man, what's this guy got that does this to me? I drain my beer. He takes the bottle from me and tosses it in a nearby can.

"This party sucks." He adds after a moment with a laugh, moving to lean on the rail with me.

The closeness isn't lost on me. We are almost touching. It reminds me of being tossing onto his bed and those big hands pulling my clothes off.

Did it just get hot out here?

"Her mother-in-law wanted it like this I think. Low-key fancy."

He nods. "Yeah, I know her. I was lured by food and free beer," he laughs.

"Caroline said she needs me for support. Not that I'm doing anything." I shrug.

"Just having a friend here probably helps. I'd say let's take off, but it sounds like you're stuck."

I glance at him out of the corner of my eye, finding him fiddling with his beer bottle. *Did he just suggest leaving with me?* Guess there's a shot for this after all. I smile to myself.

"I think I am. But at least I have someone to talk to now instead of following her around like a puppy."

When I look up again he's watching me. Our eyes meet for a moment and my stomach curls. I was an idiot to leave the first time. He's so adorable.

An hour later we are sitting at a little table across from two empty plates. Caroline peeked in at us and gave me a thumbs up, making me laugh.

"... So my dad lives here in Galveston and my sister's family lives in Austin. My mom died from cancer when I was a kid. So, it's just me and dad here." He leans back.

"Are you close at all?"

"Sort of in the middle. My sister and I talk on the phone, mostly. We usually go up there for Christmas at her house, me and dad. We catch up on the drive."

"I left home the second I turned eighteen. I was adopted by parents that shouldn't have ever been able to adopt. They were awful. I haven't seen them since."

"You're twenty-six, right? Do you miss your family?"

I nod. "Yep. I'm okay with it. I'd rather be on my own than settle for a crap relationship just to have something to hold onto." I lean forward, propped up on my hand.

"That's strong. I like that. So many people are afraid of being alone."

"I've never understood it. People come and go, it's nothing to be afraid of." I stand up. "Let's go find some cake."

He follows with a grin. "Lead the way."

The party wears on. I bounce between Caroline and Isaiah all evening until I see guests starting to leave. She wishes me luck when I tell her I'm leaving.

"Crazy. I'm not leaving with him."

"Even so. He's going to want to call you."

Man, I hope so. Given our history, I know that I'll have to bring it up and I'm perfectly okay with that.

I walk out onto the oversized front porch to find him lingering. Seeing me, he gives me a smile and casually walks me to my car.

"So," I lean on the back of my car. "Do you still have my number?"

He shoves his hands into his pockets with a crooked smirk. "I sure do."

"Use it."

Our eyes meet and I can't help but smile at him. I see the hint of memories floating in his eyes, just like they are in the back of my head every time I look up at him. He's got the same look on his face that I caught so many times when we were walking around the rodeo that day.

"I will."

I'm still standing out here long after everyone is gone, giggling at him like a school girl.

"So, you don't want coffee then?" He smiles.

"Aren't you scared? Considering that I scalded you last time."

"I am a little scared. I think I have my bulletproof vest in my trunk though." He moves, leaning beside me.

I glance up at his happy face. "You're silly. It's late anyway. Coffee puts me to sleep. I'll fall asleep driving."

He leans closer. "Don't you have coffee at home? I'll follow you."

I slap his arm playfully. "I have to work in the morning. You'd have me up all night." I stand up, glancing around.

"Didn't bother you last time."

I shake my head with a giggle. "Shut up."

Tearing my eyes off his face, I look up and see a black Corvette parked not far away with windows so darkly tinted that they are almost illegal. It tickles my brain, in that way when you know you've seen something before but can't really remember where or how.

"That's weird." I mumble.

He looks around. "What's weird?"

"That car. I know I've seen it before." I nod towards the parked car down the street.

"The Corvette? You don't remember where?"

"No, but I know I have. I'm sure it's nothing."

I watch as he pulls out his cell phone. "Hey Desiree. Yeah, it's Penrose. Can you run a plate for me please... Ready... It's... John-Tom-Lincoln-five-five-five... Ok, thanks. Can you email that to me... You're a doll."

He hangs up the phone. "Know anyone named Noah Burrell?"

My mouth drops open and a cold stone settles in my stomach. "Oh my God... yeah, I do... it must be a coincidence though."

Concern flashes in his eyes. He looks up at the car as it pulls away. "Who is he?"

"Um, he's no one. A customer that comes in every day. Just this annoyingly, friendly guy that talks to me a lot. He's pretty harmless."

His brow furrows. "Have you noticed him following you around?"

I shake my head. "I've never seen him outside of the pharmacy. Maybe he lives around here somewhere. He's always telling me about how much money he has."

"No, he doesn't live near here. At least his car isn't registered here. It's registered to an upscale neighborhood outside of Katy. He comes in every day? Why?"

"Just to say hello, or so he says. He doesn't miss a day. Everyone at work teases me about him. He's around forty-five or so and he owns a business. He's always telling me about it. He showed up today as I got off. I argued with him about letting him walk me to my car in the rain because he had an umbrella. I finally gave up and let him. He's probably just friendly."

Even as I say it, something unsettling forms in my stomach. Maybe it's the look on Isaiah's face, or the way Noah mentioned Caroline today when I don't recall ever mentioning her name. Crap. The cold stone in my gut rolls, turning into a boulder. He couldn't really be following me. There has to be some other reason. *Why would someone follow me?*

"Has he ever said anything weird to you? Made you uncomfortable?"

I look up at Isaiah, realizing that he's slipped into cop mode. He stands with his brow furrowed, arms crossed. "He's just generally creepy. Nothing you can really pinpoint. He did say something today though. I thought it was nothing. There must be an explanation." I tell him about what he said about Caroline.

Isaiah sighs. "Sounds like something's up. I'll look into it tomorrow when I get to work and I'll call you. Let me follow you home tonight, okay?"

"You really think that's necessary?" I hear the alarm in my own voice.

"It's never a bad idea to be extra careful. You never know with people, believe me. Someone can seem totally harmless and they are the farthest thing from it."

Isaiah walks back into my living room. It's strange to see him here, standing in my house. He insisted on checking it for me. He's checked all the rooms, doors, and windows. Now he meets my eyes with a sigh.

Man, I wish I'd cleaned up. He hasn't said anything, or even seemed to notice. He'd have to be blind not to notice. I'm such a slob.

"Well, I don't see anything that seems odd. Are you sure you don't want me to sleep on the couch, just in case? I don't mind. I'm not comfortable leaving you here alone if someone is following you around."

Maxie sniffs at his boots. He glances down, and she growls lightly at him.

"I'll be fine. Everything's locked. I don't think it's that serious. I doubt he's actually following me. Maybe he was just passing by and recognized me from the street or something."

"Let's hope that's all it is. Just promise me you'll call me if anything happens. I don't live too far from here. I can have cops here in a second. If you get scared, call me."

I nod. Some unseen force pulls my eyes upwards, locking on his.

"Promise me," he says, quietly.

"Okay, I promise." The warmth and worry in his eyes liquefies my brain for a second. I shake it off before speaking again. "What do I say to him when he shows up tomorrow?"

"Don't mention you saw him. But tell him you have a boyfriend. You can use my name if you need to. See if that does anything. Keep me updated okay? Keep your eyes open, know where you are and who's around you. I'll be checking on you until I figure out what's going on."

"I will. Thanks. It's probably nothing."

"Maybe it is nothing, but I've seen too much over the years to assume. Act like it's not, but hope that it is."

I follow him to the front door as he pulls his keys out of his pocket.

"Night, hey I'm glad that we ran into each other tonight." He smiles.

Something familiar in my chest flutters. "Yeah, me too. It was weird at first, but I'm glad we talked."

He bends down and Maxie sniffs his fingers, ducking away from his hand.

"Night little pup."

I grin. *A guy that talks to my dog?* Ugh, there goes my chest again.

We say our goodnights and I lock the door, checking it twice before going to bed.

CHAPTER 4

NOAH

I set my coffee cup down too hard on my desk, sloshing the black liquid all over the calendar. "Damn it." I jump up.

My partner Alex eyes me. "What's wrong with you today?"

I dab the mess with the paper towels from my bottom drawer. "Nothing, I'm fine," I snap.

He laughs at me as I toss the wad into the trash. "Fight with your girlfriend last night or something?"

I shake my head. "No, Emily is just fine. I'm just a little tired. I was up too late and that damn conference call pissed me off."

He crosses his arms as I call my secretary and ask her for more coffee and a new calendar.

"When are we going to meet her anyways? You never bring her to anything. I'm starting to wonder if she's imaginary." He guffaws at his own stupid joke.

"After the engagement I'll start to bring her to functions." I pull my top drawer out and pick up the box inside. A platinum, Tiffany engagement ring waiting for her finger.

Alex whistles. "You don't play around do you? When are you going to ask her?"

I smile, putting the ring back in the drawer. "Soon. I can't wait to see her face when she sees this ring. We are going to elope to Vegas."

"Don't you think she'll want the wedding? They all do. And what about your family?"

I look at him, glaring. "You know better than to ask me about my family." My loving family. My mother had me committed as a teenager. My brother tried to get power of attorney. All they care about now is my money. "I haven't talked to them in years."

"Regardless, she will want a wedding. Something huge and expensive no doubt. They all hemorrhage money at weddings." He rolls his eyes.

I nod. Of course she will, but I need to be married to her. After that, she can have anything she wants as long as I'm the one giving it to her.

"Yes, of course. When we get back we'll have a big party, and then plan out the wedding together. I think she's going to love it. I don't care what it costs."

He nods. "Is that why you took off all that time you have coming up?"

I smile at him. "Well, why would I want to sit here with you when I can be with her? I need a break anyway."

"How long have you two been seeing each other? Seems a bit sudden for a proposal."

I shoot him a look across the desk and he only laughs at me.

"I met her five months ago. It's never too soon when you know. What do you know. You don't even want to be married to your wife now, and she's your third. Don't talk to me about proposing. You can't seem to stop."

He laughs, nodding in agreement. "Yeah, don't remind me. Next time I want to marry one, please, find a way to stop me."

After being spotted that night, I decided to push back my plans a few days. Let things settle, just in case. There was also that guy she was talking to. I haven't been able to figure out who he is just yet.

It doesn't really matter who he is. She's going to be so happy when

I tell her what I've got planned and how I've been watching over her. Whoever that guy is, she'll forget all about him.

Today is the day. After pushing things back, I decided this morning that I wouldn't wait any longer. I'm going to see her, and, if everything goes like I think it will, she'll know that I'm the only one that can really take care of her when this is over.

It's essential that she learns to depend on me.

I rise from my desk. Alex blows out a breath and heaves his enormous frame out of the leather chair opposite me.

"Dinner?" He walks towards the door.

"Not today, I have plans."

It's not a long drive. I know all the shortcuts. If there's a way to get to this CVS I know it like the back of my hand, just like the routes to her house.

I park my Corvette up front this time. Normally, I park out of sight, but today things are different.

Right on time, I see her head towards the exit with her keys already in her hand. I get out of my car just as she walks out.

Emily sees me, recognition lights her brown eyes and a smile flashes across her face. She always smiles when she sees me. That's how I know she's glad I'm here.

"Hi there. I got your message, I'm sorry you were worried."

Confusion wrinkles her forehead, stopping her in the middle of the parking lot. "I didn't leave you a message."

I pull out my phone. "It's ok, don't be embarrassed. After seeing me every day you must have wondered what happened when I wasn't here for days."

I pull up a text sent to me by Caroline. Turning the phone, I show her the message.

Emily is asking about you. Didn't you tell her you were out of town?"

No, it was a last-minute emergency. I didn't have time. I'll be back tomorrow. I'll talk to her then.

Emily stares at it, shaking her head. "I never asked about you. You've been here every day. What are you talking about? And why are you texting my friends?"

I furrow my brow with concern. "No, sweetheart I've been in California. Are you alright?" I move to touch her arm, but she jerks out of reach. "Maybe you should sit down. Caroline is my sister, you know that."

She touches her forehead, glancing around. "I'm fine. I know you were here. I saw you and we talked. What do you mean, sister? She never mentioned a brother to me."

I frown. "Are you sure you're okay? Can I get you some water? You really don't remember?"

She shakes her head. "No, I'm fine. I don't know what's going on here, but if it's a sick joke it's not funny."

She pushes past me, headed for her car. "Emily, I'd never do that to you. Hey, take this." I hold out my card. "Call me if you need anything. I'm worried about you."

She takes the card, shaking her head, and then gets into her car and slams the door.

If she depends on me, she'll realize how much she loves me. I only have to make her see it.

No one can love Emily the way I do.

After she drives away, I walk back towards my car and dial Caroline's number.

EMILY

I toss the card into the cup holder. I know I saw him.

Suddenly, my head is throbbing.

This has to be a joke. Noah's screwed up sense of humor or something. I'm going to call Caroline and get to the bottom of this.

When I get home I change into yoga pants and a t-shirt. After hooking Maxie's leash on her collar, I put my Bluetooth on my ear, head out for a walk, and I dial Caroline number.

"Hey girl, what up."

"Hi. Um… you know Noah Burrell?" No point in beating around the bush I guess. Her laugh sounds in my head, light and rolling, confusing me.

"You're so funny. Do I know him? As if I wouldn't know my own brother." She sounds certain and happy.

Brother? Noah is her brother? Since when does she have a brother? In two years, not a peep. Confused by this information, I reach back into my memory for anything that would have suggested this. Something to give me a hint as to why she seems to think I know what in the hell she's talking about, but I find nothing. I don't remember any of this. Something has to be wrong here.

"I don't remember that. He shows up at my work every day… he…

I don't remember you ever mentioning even having a brother." I falter. *What do I even say?*

"You called me two days ago asking about him. You're friends, right? Why else would you be worried about him?"

My head starts to throb. "No, I didn't. I never called you and he's not my friend. What the hell are you talking about?" I shout. I draw the attention of an elderly woman watering her roses.

"Why are you yelling? Are you okay? I can't believe you don't remember."

"Why would I do that? He's weird and creepy. And besides, he's been at my work every day for months. He never went anywhere. Are you two playing some joke on me?"

The line is silent for a moment.

"He might be a little off beat, but I think creepy is a stretch. Are you okay?"

"No, I'm not okay," I shout, waving my arm. My dog looks up at me. "You're dropping this bomb on me and acting like I'm some loon. I don't remember any of this. You've got to be messing with me." Surely, this is some elaborate joke.

"Emily, you're freaking me out here. I think maybe you need some rest and you'll feel better." Her voice is thick with concern.

I stop walking. Okay, maybe it's not a joke. I swallow, but my mouth is suddenly dry. Maxie bends and sniffs a patch of grass. "I'm not crazy."

"I think you're just tired. Get some rest and I'll talk to you later. I'm sure you'll feel better. Maybe you should call Noah and have him come check on you."

I feel sick. *Why would she think that I would do such a thing?* Bile rises in my throat, burning me as I swallow the bitterness back down. I tug on Maxie's leash. "Why would I call him? I told you that he's been bothering me. I didn't even have his number until today when he gave me his card. I don't even know him."

She sighs. "Are you really asking me this? Are you playing with me? You're scaring me Emily." Her voice is soft.

I'm scaring her? I'm the one standing here on the corner shaking, ready to throw up.

"I don't know what you're talking about Caroline. And leave Noah out of this."

"Get some rest, okay? I'll call you tomorrow. And call Noah. I know he works a lot, but you know that he'll be there for you for whatever this is."

I hang up, my fingers shaking. I feel fine, except for my throbbing headache. *How can this be?* I don't remember any of this. I remember worrying all week about this nut following me around. I remember looking over my shoulder everywhere I went in case that black Corvette was lurking. I have been double checking the locks on my doors and looking into the backseat of my car.

I haven't seen him again, except for when he shows up at my job. Of course, now he's saying he wasn't there. Someone at the store had to have seen him, right? *I'm not losing it, am I?*

Maxie and I head back home. I need a distraction. When I walk in my front door, I release Maxie from her leash and toss it on the floor. My keys go back in the bowl.

Isaiah crosses my mind. We've talked on the phone several times, but we haven't made any plans to meet. He's been busy and out of town for work. I could tell him what's going on. No, bad idea. *What if it really is me?* I don't want him to look at me all weird and thinking something is going on.

Hell, I couldn't really be this confused, could I? I glance down at my dog with a sigh. *What is happening to me?*

I need to clean my house. That ought to keep me too busy to worry about this. There is clean laundry piled up on my white, leather couch. My shoes are scattered everywhere across the hardwood floor. Dog hair is on my area rug, which I need to vacuum. There are coffee mugs on the coffee table and end tables. Then there is the kitchen. My counters are piled up with dishes, both clean and dirty. I blow out a breath. I'm not a pig, but sloppy and I are good friends.

After two hours of picking up, doing laundry, washing dishes, and wiping counters, I turn on my Keurig and brew my nightly cup of coffee. Coffee before bed makes me sleep, oddly enough. My nightly routine is a big, creamy mug of java and whatever shows I have recorded in my DVR.

I lay my clothes out for work tomorrow, slip into my clean sheets, and tell myself today was just a bad day. Maxie jumps up onto the bed beside me, laying down in her usual spot.

Tomorrow will be a better day.

The blare of my alarm clock is always a brutal good morning. With a groan, I turn it off and stretch.

"Morning Maxie." I scratch her head as my feet hit the cold, hardwood floor in my bedroom.

I kick clothes out of the way as I trek through the mess towards the bathroom, and then I freeze. *Didn't I clean this up?* I spin in my room. It's a mess. My heart starts to pound as I push my fingers into my hair.

What the hell is going on? I move to the living room. It's as cluttered as ever. My sink is full of dishes that I remember loading into the dishwasher last night. *Am I losing my damn mind?* I spin again, blinking my eyes and opening them with the futile hope that this is a dream that can be blinked away.

No luck.

With no idea of what to do, I head back to my bedroom. My clothes are laid out on my chair, just like I remember.

Something is wrong. Tears blur my vision. *What's going on here? Why can't I remember?*

I reach into the recesses of my mind for something, anything that might explain what happened over the last twenty-four hours. I find nothing, no fuzzy memories. Nothing but another headache that threatens to split my head open.

Is this what happens when people go mad?

ISAIAH

I finally had a moment to look into this character Noah for Emily, and tonight I'm meeting her for dinner to talk about it.

As I grip my steering wheel on the way to Johnny Carrabbas, my palms are sweating. I wipe them on my jeans, reminding myself one more time that this isn't a real date.

Blowing out a breath, I park and laugh as I get out of my car. What a joke. My mouth is dry and I know it's because, in a minute, I'll be looking into those brown eyes and cracking jokes to see that smile on those lips.

I'm torn. We've been flirting, but she's never come right out and suggested we go on an actual date, and I'll be damned if I'm going to make the first move after what happened. I'm glad to be seeing her again, but I can't help but be worried she might freak out and take off on me once things heat up. I don't know who I'm fooling. I know as soon as I see her, all reason will go out the window.

After thanking the hostess, I spot her sitting alone at a table for two sipping on water. She waves at me from across the room, and I grin. She glances at the gun on my hip and the badge embroidered on my polo. I came straight from work.

This is not a date. I tell myself again as I sit down, picking up the menu without seeing it.

"Hey, waiting long?" I look over the menu, forcing myself to pay attention to what I'm reading.

"No, no I just got here."

"How's everything? Any more trouble?" I set the menu down and shove it aside.

Her eyes are troubled. Her smile flickers like a flame in the wind.

"Nothing to speak of."

She's holding back something. At thirty years old, I've been a cop for almost one-third of my life. I can spot a lie. I can't hold it against her because it's not like we know each other all that well. Just because I've seen her naked doesn't mean she is obligated to share with me, but I want her to. The waitress arrives and Emily orders the Chicken Bryan, and I order plain lasagna and salad.

"Well, I wasn't able to find much. He's forty-three years old, not married. No criminal history, a few traffic tickets. Nothing I could find makes him stand out, but that doesn't mean anything. He might be good at flying under the radar. Not to mention he knows half the cops in the whole county since he owns Blue Liners, which is where they all buy their gear. Have you seen him lately?"

She nods. "Yep. He doesn't miss a day."

I drum my fingers on the table. She chews on her lip.

"I'm sorry I couldn't find out more. I couldn't justify digging any deeper without getting into trouble or harassing him."

"I know, I appreciate what you did. Just, this is so... frustrating. I wonder if I should just ask him right out if he followed me."

"I honestly don't know. That could backfire."

"Which is precisely why I haven't. It can't last forever I suppose. Maybe eventually he'll get bored and move on."

Last week she was sure that it was a coincidence. Now she doesn't seem so confident.

"Has something else happened? You seem more bothered by it now than you were a week ago."

She shakes her head without looking at me. "Nothing to speak of."

This again. It tells me that there is something and she just won't say. Maybe she just needs more time. Perhaps if we spend more time together she will feel more secure talking to me. I take a drink of my ice water and watch how she avoids my eyes.

"Hey, why don't you let me teach you how to handle a gun?"

She looks up with wide eyes. "What? I've never even held a gun before. You think it's that bad?"

"I don't know. But I'm a believer in self-preservation. It can't hurt to know how to defend yourself. We can go tomorrow. I'll let you borrow one of mine. I have a smaller pistol you can handle."

I can't imagine what she's thinking. For all I know she's one of those I hate guns no matter what people. At least if she learns how to do the basics, I'll feel a bit more at ease with this weirdo on the loose.

"I don't know, is it hard?"

The innocence in her face makes me smile. "Not really. Most idiots can handle a gun. So, you should be fine."

She laughs, relaxing a little. "So, I'm most idiots?"

"Naw, you're a special breed." I wink.

She laughs again, meeting my eyes. "Well, you're a special kind of idiot yourself."

"At least we're on the same page. So, tomorrow?"

She considers me carefully for a moment before she says, "Alright. I'm off tomorrow. What's a good time?"

I grin. "I'll pick you up around noon. You'll be an expert marksman when I get done with you."

"Yeah, right." She laughs as our food comes.

Whatever she was thinking about must be forgotten now. She's smiling at me as she eats and laughing at my stupid jokes. She orders a dessert and we share it, eating slowly. Somehow, I get the feeling she feels like I do and isn't quite ready to leave yet.

When I walk her to her car, I have to shove my hands into my pockets to keep from touching her. Emily brushes her hair off of her face, turning her eyes up to me. I'm dying to see her glittering brown eyes drift close as I lean into her lips. Instead, I smile as she fishes her keys out of an oversized purse.

"Thanks for dinner, Isaiah. I guess I'll see you tomorrow."

"Have a good night, and your welcome. I had a good time."

She smiles. "So did I."

Silence hangs between us as she stares up at me. After a moment, she takes a deep breath, clicks her key fob, and opens her door.

"See you." She grins as she gets into her car.

I wiggle my fingers in a wave, backing up. "Bye girl."

CHAPTER 5

ISAIAH

Emily stares down at the small pistol in her hands with wide eyes as if it's going to bite her. We're at an outdoor gun range. The sun is bright and there isn't a cloud in the sky. She has her red hair pulled back in a ponytail. A green t-shirt brings out her eyes, topping jean shorts.

"How's it feel?" I ask.

She shrugs.

I show her how to load it and unload it. I show her the safety. I make her load and unload it three times, and I make her show me where the safety is over and over again.

"Shoot to kill. There's no such thing as shooting in the leg or in the hand like in the movies. This is real life, and if you point a gun at someone it's because you want to kill them. Got it?"

"Yes." Her voice is quiet.

I take the gun from her and hand her ear protection. "Watch me."

I take my stance. Glancing over at her, I see she's watching with intensity and appears to be studying me. After I pop off a few rounds, I change out the paper target for a fresh one.

"Ready?"

"As I'll ever be." She blows out a breath.

"Like this." I move behind her, ordering her foot placement. I put my arms over hers, gripping her hands in mine. Damn, she's right against my chest and her hair brushes my neck as I lean over to speak to her. God, she smells good. "How's it feel?"

She turns her head, meeting my eyes. She's so close I could kiss her by just moving an inch.

"Better than I expected it to." Her eyes glitter.

I grin. *Is she talking about me or the gun?*

"Fire when ready." I let her go, backing up.

She inhales and exhales, glancing back at me with a flash of determination on her face. She mumbles something I can't hear and then shoots. She lets four rounds go off in quick succession and then turns to me with a smile and sets the gun down.

I push the button, bringing the target in for inspection. "Look, you got him once in the stomach."

She yells, clapping. Her outburst scares the hell out of me. Then she throws her arms around me in a warm embrace. "I did it!"

I smile down into her face, my arms around her waist. "You sure did. Good job. Wanna go again?"

Emily looks up into my eyes in a way that makes my chest tight. Her eyes glance over my face. "Yes, please."

Well, hell. She isn't letting go and neither am I. For a long moment I absorb the heat from her body, remembering things that I shouldn't be thinking about right now. Her smile broadens and she slips out of my arms with a giggle.

I have to keep reminding myself that I can't make the first move. I run my hand through my hair as she positions herself to shoot again.

About an hour later, I pull the bag I brought with me out of the trunk of my car. She puts on sunglasses as I circle around in the parking lot of the range, calling her name.

Setting the black duffel on the hood of the car, I motion to her. "Hey, come here. I've got something for you."

She gives me a crooked smile and approaches with a bounce in her step. I slide the bag over.

With the slow sound of a zipper, she opens it. Her mouth falls open and bright, wide eyes turn up to mine. "The stuffed animals? From the carnival?"

I smile as she pulls them out one by one. "I thought you might want them." Hopefully she won't think I'm weird for keeping them all this time.

"You kept them all this time?" She clutches a pink stuffed pig to her chest and turns to me.

"Yeah. Is that weird?" I wince.

She grins. "No, no it's not. It's so sweet. I'm so glad you kept them. Thank you."

Our eyes meet and she steps into me like she did that night at the rodeo.

"Your welcome." I manage after a moment.

Raising her sunglasses, she gives me a view of her eyes that catches my breath. Her free hand finds my arm, the touch sending heat from my forearm upwards. In that moment, she pops up on her toes and kisses me. I think she intended a peck, but I catch her around the waist and she melts immediately. Her hands move to my face as she opens her mouth, inviting my tongue, and it's accepted with a sigh. Her kiss is sweet and slow, and intoxicating. I didn't think it possible, but it's even better than I remember. I fist the back of her shirt. She pulls my mouth into hers for a kiss so slow and deep that I can't even remember my own name.

Breaking our lips apart, we smile at the same time. "So, lunch?"

She nods. "Sounds good."

I'm grabbed by the front of my shirt and pulled down into her lips, where I grin against her and she giggles. "I missed you." I mutter against her mouth.

"Me too. I was so stupid."

"You really were. Seems you've come to your senses."

She laughs, as her mouth covers mine, and she pinches my arm. I yelp. "Ow!"

Another giggle when I smack her ass. *Damn how could I have missed her this much after only one date?* Whatever the reason, seems I've got her back.

NOAH

I've been waiting for Emily to come home. I was prepared to follow her around today on her day off, but when I got here she was already gone. Normally, knowing she doesn't work the following day, I'd spend the night in the attic and enjoy the leisurely morning with her, but last night I wasn't able to.

The hours tick by and I haven't seen a sign of her.

I hear the front door around eight and my heart jumps. Peering through the hole into the living area, I watch from above. She's smiling, wearing a green t-shirt and shorts. Her purse is tossed onto the couch.

Where have you been all day, my love?

I've been working on my plans all week. Upsetting her world little by little, just enough to make her wonder. Making her question what's really happening around her, and who she can turn to for help. I hate to upset her, but it's the only way I can bring her close and make her dependent. I must be her rock, and this is the best way.

I know in the end, she will thank me.

She moves out of view, I head carefully to the next hole. I find her in the bathroom. Careful not to make a sound, I lay on the attic floor watching her. She sits on the edge of the tub, turning on the bath and adjusting the temperature. She adds bubbles and bath oil. Next, she turns on the radio that's on the counter. The sound of twangy country music assaults my ears, but I ignore it.

Emily takes off her shorts first, wiggling out of them as she kicks off her shoes. Both are tossed aside. My breathing picks up as I watch her grip the hem of her t-shirt, slowly pulling it over her head. Now standing in just a pink demi-cup bra and matching thong panties. She knows what I like, teasing me this way. Undressing slowly, bending to check the water so that I catch a perfect view of her from behind.

Holding my breath, I watch her breasts come tumbling out as she slips out of the bra. The panties are next. My heart is thundering when she slips into the tub, pinning her red hair up as she sinks into the bubbles. Stretching in the water, she gives me a glorious view before sinking further into the water, her curves tickled by bubbles as they move out of sight.

It's not the first time I've watched her in the tub. It always takes everything I have to control my breathing, careful not to move or make noise as I watch her slip her hands over her body, lathering, and shaving. Moving slowly, she knows how I love to watch.

My breath catches when she slips her hand into the water and her thighs fall apart. My breath comes heavier as I watch her hand move, the bubbles disappearing just enough to let me see her fingers work. Her mouth opens and she bites her lip.

She likes it when I'm watching. Because she's a good girl, she wants to please me.

Soon we will be together, very soon. The thought of touching her, the softness of her thighs and the way she breathes when she's excited, it makes me light headed.

She's going to be so happy.

I watch her until she falls asleep. Even then, I wait a while before daring to venture out of the attic. Her house is newer, so it has stairs instead of the ladder that most houses have, making it much easier and quieter to get out.

I wouldn't want to wake her. She needs her rest. But, now it's time to get to work. First thing, I crank the air conditioner down to fifty-eight degrees. I've never once seen her touch it, in these last few months. She keeps her house at seventy-four degrees, day and night.

Unable to resist, I slip into her room. She's sleeping naked again. The blankets have slipped down to her waist as she lays on her back, her bare breasts rise and fall in the slow deep rhythm of sleep. One leg sticks out from under the blankets.

Sleep well, my lovely. I can't wait to be with you.

CHAPTER 6

EMILY

Emily. Wake up Emily, I love you, angel.

I bolt up in bed. *What the fuck was that? Did I dream that?* My ears still ring from the whispers echoing in my brain. Clutching the blankets to my body the freezing cold hits me. *Why is it cold*?

I glance around the room, terrified of the shadows. Everything looks normal. Surely, it was just a dream. Blowing out a breath, I get out of bed and wrap a blanket around me. Maxie lifts her sleepy head from the pillow, watching me move around my room, checking under my bed and in the closet. Nothing. She would be barking if anyone was here. I'm being silly.

Maybe I should check the rest of the house, just in case. I shuffle from room to room. Everything looks fine. There is no one lurking, and I hear no more voices. It must have been a dream, but damn if it felt like one. I was dead asleep and hear what sounds like a voice next to my bed. Maybe it wasn't a dream.

A dull throb is starting in the back of my head. I swear. Not another freaking headache. I shake my head, shuffling to the bathroom to pop some more Advil.

I stop in the hallway and check the thermostat. It's set to fifty-eight. "What the hell, I didn't change this." I mutter, changing it back.

There is no one else here. It had to be me that changed it. *God, what's wrong with me?* I thought the headaches were from the stress, but maybe I have a tumor or something.

This shit's been happening all week. I got gas the other night on my way home. The next morning my tank was on E again.

I went to work on Wednesday. They all looked at me weird and told me that I had called in sick the night before. I don't remember calling.

Caroline showed up to check on me and asked me how things were since I've started dating Noah. I tried to explain to her, but she looked at me like I've lost my ever-loving mind. I even went back to find the business card he gave me, to show her that I barely know him. I couldn't find it. I told her that I've started dating Isaiah again, and she laughed at me and said, "What Noah doesn't know won't hurt him." She thinks that I'm seeing both of them at the same time and, despite my arguments, she swore to keep my secret from them both. After several minutes, I finally gave up and made an excuse to get her to leave. What's the point in talking to someone that isn't listening and acts like I've got one foot in the door of the asylum?

Now I'm having nightmares. Voices are waking me up in the middle of the night. At least I'm not hearing them during the day. Not yet, anyway.

I get back into bed, but I can't sleep. Every little sound perks my ears and makes my head turn. I burrow further under the blankets, as if they can protect me.

I let my mind drift to Isaiah, his smiling kisses and stupid jokes. I wish I could call him, but it's three in the morning. He'd have a heart attack if I woke him up, especially if it was to tell him I had a bad dream.

I'm afraid to tell him about what's going on. The last thing I want, after finding him again, is to scare him off by making him think that I'm losing my marbles.

There has to be some rational explanation for this. Tomorrow I'm going to his apartment for dinner. He wants to cook for me. The thought makes me smile. Slowly, my fear melts into something warm and I drift back to sleep dreaming of Isaiah.

NOTHING SPECTACULAR HAPPENS ALL DAY. I'm lulled slowly into a sense of *everything is okay* as I count the time down to my date.

No weirdness, no headaches.

I spend the day cleaning up and ignoring text messages from Caroline. She's the last person I want to talk to right now. She's only confusing me further. I never thought I'd be one to doubt my own senses, but after I talk to her I always do.

I dress in a wraparound pencil skirt in burgundy, a white lace form fitting top with a deep enough neckline to show off my cleavage, and high heels. I tousle my hair, and I'm out the door.

"Don't wait up Maxie." I blow my dog a kiss.

Twenty minutes later I'm knocking on his door. The same door I remember being pressed up against months ago in a breathless kiss. The door opens and I'm faced with a handsome, smiling blond wearing charcoal dress pants and a deep blue shirt. His cologne wafts out as he looks me over.

"Hey beautiful." He steps aside to let me in.

The scent of Mexican food hits my nose and makes my mouth water.

"Hi handsome. What's cooking?"

He smiles, closing the door as I turn in the room. It's just as I remember it. Clean and manly. He's so much tidier than I am. "Your apartment is so pretty, and this view is simply amazing." I sigh, walking over to the big window that overlooks the woods.

I feel his body come up behind me, and he places his hands on my hips. "Thank you. I'm glad you like it. Are you hungry?"

I nod. "I'm starving. Do you like to cook? Or is this special just for me?" I turn to face him.

He gazes happily down at me. "Yes, ma'am. I sure do. You look stunning, by the way."

I bite my lip and tilt my head. "Thank you. So, what's for dinner?"

Isaiah pulls me into his arms, which he circles around my waist. "Fajitas and rice. *Dulce le leche* for dessert."

I smile, touching the buttons on his shirt. My pulse picks up as I take in the feel of his strong body and the delicious way he smells. I told myself today that I wouldn't sleep with him tonight. Despite this, I picked out special panties and a matching bra. As I carefully dressed, dreaming of his hands undressing me, I said, *not tonight*.

I've asked myself if I'd think differently if so many weird things had not been happening, but in my head I decided before I left not to jump into his bed so soon. What if something strange happens while I'm here? *At least I'd have a witness, and maybe some answers.*

But the soft way he's looking at me with these copper brown eyes, his arms curled around me making my skin feel electrified is making me glad that I took careful care picking out my underwear.

He bends, nuzzling his nose to mine. I grin. He makes me feel like I've known him forever. This connection is amazing. What had me scared before, has me excited this time.

"Let's eat." He takes my hand and leads me across the room to a set table. The table is round, made of white oak with four gray padded chairs around it. He's got two candles flickering in the center. He turns down the lights. I smile as he pulls my chair out for me. I watch him with a palpitating heart as he walks into the kitchen and retrieves a bottle of white wine and pours two glasses.

After handing me a glass, he heads back to the kitchen and returns with two plates of steaming Mexican food.

"Isaiah, this is amazing." I inhale a deep breath of the spicy scent.

"Well, dig in."

We talk and eat and laugh. He refills my glass and brings me cake that melts in my mouth and we laugh and talk more. Eventually, I find myself barefoot in his kitchen helping him wash dishes. I've forgotten all the things that I've been so worried about all week long. I stand at the sink giggling at his jokes and listening to his stories as if nothing has happened.

"It took me years to get this place decorated like I wanted. I got furniture bit by bit, so it looks like I spent a fortune." He laughs.

I close the door on the dishwasher and turn it on. A low hum fills the room under the sound of the soft music playing.

"It's gorgeous. I don't have the eye for this to decorate my place. It's a mess."

He follows me into the living area, where I sit with my legs tucked under me on the couch.

"Your house is nice." He touches my hair. I scoot closer to him.

I look into his eyes, knowing I'm never going to be able to tell him no. The minute I feel his hands on me I'll be lost. I should get up and go home, but lately home is a little scary. Maybe here I can pull my head back together and settle my soul a little. I'd like to be a little bit lost with him.

"Do you want more wine?" he asks, softly.

"No, thanks. I'm perfect."

He smiles. "You really are."

I laugh at his cheesy line. He leans in closer. His lips are soft, tasting faintly of the wine. Slow, nibbling kisses that slowly deepen are my favorite, and he doesn't disappoint. I rise up on my knees, and his arms pull me in tight as he tickles my lips, teasing me with his tongue. Grabbing him by his collar, I pull him in closer and he groans as our tongues tangle and tease each other.

Before long I'm on my back, his lips on my throat, and his hands tugging at the hem of my shirt to gain access to more skin. We take our time, luxuriating in the slow removal of clothes and lips that linger and explore inch by inch. Soon the room is filled with sighs and soft moans.

My legs are wrapped around his hips. This time isn't like last time. Last time was hot and furious. We were crazed by the heat we generated, which drove us into virtual madness together. This time it's measured, and we enjoy every slow moment. I look up, reaching and brushing the hair off his face as he loves me. He catches my palm in a kiss, his gaze is soft as he looks deeply into my eyes. I gasp from the roll of his hips into mine.

He says my name against my lips in a whisper when it's done. Still resting between my legs lazily on the couch, he kisses me again. "Stay."

The single word on his lips catches in my chest. "Okay. Will you make me breakfast?"

He smiles, and his eyes dance across my face. "I will. I think you're amazing, Emily."

"I'm so glad I found you again," I confess. I never should have left this man.

He kisses my nose, my lips, my ear. I turn my head and look into tender eyes, falling into them.

"Come to bed with me."

"Lead the way."

CHAPTER 7

ISAIAH

She stayed. I grin as Emily curls into me sleepily in the morning light as it shines into my bedroom.

"Morning, sexy," she purrs with her lips on my neck and a giggle in my ear.

Rolling up on my side, I kiss smiling lips. "Morning yourself. How did you sleep?"

Her eyes drift closed as she closes in for another kiss. "Best sleep in weeks." She slings a frisky leg over my hip.

I graze her thigh and hip with my hand, as she presses soft curves against by body.

"Mmm," I smile.

She bites her lip. "Do you have plans today?"

"Just with you."

Her smile is coupled with glittering eyes. I want to know everything about the woman that has so fully captured me. There are so many questions that I have for her, but I can't stop myself from pulling her on top of me after I roll onto my back. Her hair falls around my face as she leans over me, tracing her fingers over my chest.

I push my hand into her hair, running my fingers through the silkiness.

"Tell me about your family."

She sighs as she sits up, giving me a glorious view of her naked body. I slip my hand over her throat and down her body in a slow caress.

"My family? I don't really have one. We're scattered to the Four Winds. I don't even think about them anymore. I told you about the adoption."

"What happened when you left home?"

"I moved in with my friend from school, Laura. We got jobs and worked through school. She was killed in a car accident about three years ago."

I didn't realize she had such a tragic past. I pull my eyes off her body and up to her face. She's not upset. She talks about it as if it's nothing.

"Wow, that's horrible. So you—"

"Live alone? No family? Yeah, that's me. It's okay. I prefer it to being with awful people. I dealt with it a long time ago."

I smile, and my hands move over her hips. "You want the real thing, and you won't settle for anything less?"

Leaning over me, she nods. "Yes. I hang out with people from work sometimes. I used to talk to Caroline a lot, but..." She doesn't finish. Her eyes cloud and she sighs.

"But what?"

"Nothing. It's nothing. Why are we talking about this?" She nuzzles my nose.

"I want to know everything about you," I mutter, between kisses.

"Well, I never knew my birth parents. My mom is this abusive woman who never should have had kids. She used to scream at me for everything. My dad was a bum who didn't like to work. He spent all day on the beach surfing. It wasn't super bad, but it wasn't good either. I always told myself that I'd do better than that. One day I would be something that I could be proud of, that my kids could be proud of."

She slips off of me and settles back on my shoulder. *Does she have trouble getting close to people? Are there trust issues?* I guess that's why she freaked out the first time.

"What about your family?"

Her voice pulls me back to her face.

"It must have been awful to lose your mom that way," she continues.

I shrug. "Yeah, it was bad. Took a long time for me and my sister to recover from losing her. My mom was an amazing woman. But like you said, life goes on."

I almost tell her that I'll take her to meet them all, my family, someday, but I don't. I also almost ask her how many kids she wants, but I swallow that question down too. Instead I get up.

"What do you want for breakfast?"

Her eyes drift over my body lazily, making me smile. "Surprise me."

As I pull on a pair of gray sweatpants, her phone rings in the living room. I run to grab it, notice there is just a number on the screen, and toss it to her. She smiles and answers. "Hello... How did you get this number?" Her face goes white. "No, no I didn't... Look, this has gone on long enough..."

She looks up at me with tears in her eyes. "It's him. He's calling me."

With a frown, I take the phone from her. "Hello, who is this?"

"Um, this is Noah, who is this? I was talking to Emily."

I look down at her, and see tears rolling down her cheeks.

"This is Detective Penrose with Katy Police. Miss Bronte has advised me that you are harassing her."

Noah coughs. "Harassing her? No, I'm not harassing her. Detective, I appreciate what you're doing but there are things you don't know about Emily—"

I cut him off, not willing to listen to any of his crap. "No, you listen. If you refuse to stop contacting her, I'll be forced to contact the district attorney's office and pursue charges. Do you understand me?"

He laughs, a light chuckle. "Yes, officer. I understand you perfectly."

"Good. Is there anything else that I can do for you?"

"No." The line goes dead.

I look over at her. She's holding her knees to her chest, crying.

"Tell me what is going on."

Emily looks up at me with sad eyes. "You might want to sit down."

NOAH

I look down at the phone in my hand with a frown. *Why would she call the police? And where was she all night long*? It's almost noon, and she never came home last night. None of this makes sense. Emily loves me. She'd never call the police on me.

I need to know who he is, and why Emily is with him. There has to be a reason. She knows that she's mine. I can see it in her eyes when she looks at me, in her smile when she looks up into my eyes, and in the way my name comes off her lips. She's mine. There's a reasonable explanation for this. Maybe it's the stress. Perhaps I should back off the scare tactics for a day or so and let her settle a bit. I've noticed how jumpy she is. She's complaining of headaches and popping Advil. It must be stress. The last thing I want to do is hurt her.

With a deep breath, I scroll through my phone for a number I haven't called in a while. I know where to go to get more information on this Penrose. She'll help me with this. I'd drop by the police department, but, as a Detective Sergeant, she doesn't work on Sundays.

"Hello."

"Julie, it's been a while." I put a smile into my voice.

"This can't be Noah. I haven't heard from you in a long time."

"I know. I'm sorry. You know how it is, I get lost in my little world over here."

She laughs. "That's okay. I know how important that world is to you. So how have you been?"

And so the small talk goes. Catching up with her after over a year without calling her. The lack of contact doesn't stop her from flirting and dropping innuendo. Of course, I pick it up, and give it right back. A man has to do what he has to do to get things done.

When I ask her to lunch, she jumps right on it. Unfortunately, she's not in town. I have to wait until tomorrow.

I don't like to wait.

I crack my knuckles as I sit in the car, one street over from my beloved's house. Emily is worth waiting for.

EMILY

I look up into Isaiah's face, clutching the blanket to my chest. As I tell him the whole story, every screwed up detail, I cry. I'm not proud of it, but I can't seem to hold back. I pride myself on being strong, but something in the look in his eyes causes me to confess everything that has happened over the last few weeks. It's like a dam broke. At some point, he pulls me into his lap, which only makes the crying worse. I bury my face in his neck, as if it's the last time I'll get to inhale his scent, fearing he will lose my number after this.

"Honey, why didn't you tell me?" His voice is soft and sweet. He's not appalled like I expected.

"It sounds crazy. I have a hard time believing it myself."

He lifts my head, forcing my eyes to his. Warm fingers brush the damp from my cheeks. "Baby, it's not crazy. I don't think you're crazy."

He doesn't think I'm crazy. Well, that's a relief. I inhale a deep, shaky breath. "I didn't want to bother you with it. How would I even start?"

"That's what boyfriends are for."

Boyfriend. He's done it now. Something light flutters down into my chest, as if a feather had been dropped there and settled on my heart. Somehow, it eases the strain I've been under.

"You don't think it's all in my head? What could it be?"

"There's a reasonable explanation for everything, I don't doubt it one bit. Didn't you ever wonder if maybe someone was breaking into your house? Doing all this to mess with you?"

"Who would do that? And what about Caroline? She's so certain when she talks about Noah. I had no idea she even had a brother and she acts like I've always known. And the look she gives me, like she thinks I belong in a home or something. She's been my friend for two years. Why would she lie?"

"Blood is thicker than water, or so the saying goes. If they really are brother and sister, there's a million reasons. There's quite an age gap there, maybe he raised her or something. Could be she feels obligated to him or something. As far as all the weirdness at your house, didn't you ever wonder if maybe it's him, or her? He's calling you on your phone and he comes to your work and tells you that you forgot all that stuff?"

His arms tighten around my hips. I swallow. "I guess I don't want to believe it. Why me? I'm nobody special. He doesn't know me."

Astounding relief coupled with terror twists up inside me. Isaiah believes me. I'm not crazy. But that would mean Noah has been in my house, following me. A fist of ice wraps around my heart. *Is he stalking me? Would he hurt me? Oh, God. Caroline's been to my house a million times. She could have done something to allow him access.* Sudden pain hits my stomach. Sick reality forms a hard knot that cramps my guts into a knot and burns my eyes with unshed tears.

"Emily, you're assuming that he's a rational thinker. Maybe he's not. Lots of people with serious issues walk around able to function and giving no clue that something is wrong. On top of it, he has money, and lots of it. Everything you've said is easily something he could be orchestrating to screw with your head. He might have some twisted reasoning behind it, which we can't know for sure at this point. I'd have to look into his history. Hers too for that matter." His eyes are soft with concern.

Would a stranger, who doesn't even know anything about me, really be doing all of this to me?

The warmth of his hands is soothing as I breathe in what he's suggesting. He's a cop; so, he would pick up on the weirdness before I would, I suppose. Probably handles strange things every day without even blinking. He can probably smell a lie a mile away too.

"So, what should I do?" My voice is smaller than intended.

He tucks my hair out of my face. "Make a report. Change your locks. Block him from your phone. Get a weapon. Maybe it's best if you don't go home for a few days."

Not go home? What? "What do I do? Hole up in a hotel for a couple of weeks? I don't want to—"

He cuts me off with a soft kiss. "Baby, you can stay here."

"I can't just move in here for days. What if he follows me here?"

"Then I'll kick his ass. There's room for you. The bed's big enough." He smiles at me.

I can't help but smile back. Might not be the worst thing in the world, curling up next to this sexy blond for the next few days and playing house with him.

"But we just started dating. We don't even know each other very well yet."

He tilts his head. I can see the stubborn streak in him is just as wide as it is in me. It's glowing in his eyes as he grins wider at me before planting kisses on my shoulders.

"I know enough. It's not forever. You need to be in a safe place, until we know what's happening. When it blows over, you go home. I'm not willing to risk your safety now that I finally found you again." He says the last bit quietly.

A sigh comes out of me, deep and from the part of my gut that knows I can't say no to this face. Before I open my mouth, I feel the heat of his full lips on mine. An intimate invasion that makes whatever protest I was forming flutter away.

"Shut up," he mutters, taking my lips again as he opens his eyes just long enough to catch me in his hypnotic gaze. "Don't overthink it. Let me do this."

His hands on my face, nibbling kisses, and gentle nuzzles cause peace to settle deep in my soul. Isaiah is my safe place. I've got no doubts about it. I've never trusted anyone so easily before.

"Okay. I'll stay for a little bit," I whisper.

He smiles against my kiss and makes a gentle growl of pleasure when my arms go around his neck.

"Good. Let's get some breakfast in us, and then we can head over to your place get some things. We'll have a locksmith come over."

With a nod, I stand. He swats me on my bare behind as he passes me on his way to the kitchen.

In his shower, the hot water rains down on my body, washing away all the confusion. Isaiah has brought me back to myself when I thought that I might be losing it. I squirt some of his body wash into my hands. It smells clean and like him and makes me smile as I lather it onto my skin. Now I'll get to smell like him all day long.

CHAPTER 8

NOAH

I should have followed her. I always regret it when I don't. Now I've got this cop to worry about, and I've got no idea where she's been all night long.

After the phone call, I make my way back into the house. I spent the night in the attic again, waiting for her and missing her. I had my videos to keep me company, but it's not the same. I fed her dog, and we played fetch with the little yellow ball she loves so much. I'm not really into animals, but Emily will be thrilled to know I took the time to bond with her little Maxie.

When I hear the door, thankfully I'm in the attic. Body flush to the floor, I peer through the small hole with a heavy heartbeat. I've missed her. I knew she'd come home.

Looking stunning in a pencil skirt and lace top, she floats into the room. I've bought her so many clothes. I can't wait to show them to her. She deserves only the best.

I see the same blond guy from the night of the party follow her into the house, and I suck in a breath. His muffled voice floats up to my ears. "I'm going to check the house while you pack."

Shit. I get up off the floor, careful to tread lightly. No place to hide up here. Nothing to hide in or behind. Fuck. If he comes up here I'm screwed. Not even a window to get out.

Wait, he said pack. *Why is she packing? Where is she going? Damn it, who is this guy?* I've been watching her for months. There has been nothing new. There is no one that I don't know in her life. I've checked out everyone.

This blondie comes along and screws up everything. *Who the hell is he*? Maybe he's a relative. She'd never cheat on me. I know she loves me. She's waiting for me.

My thoughts start to come in a jumbled mess as I cross to one of my cameras. I hide it, with the other one under some insulation in a dark corner.

She's packing. Why is she packing?

Who is this guy?

She called the cops.

She doesn't love you.

No, she loves me. I know she does. It's in her eyes.

She's confused, or maybe he's forced her.

Where is she going? Is she going with him?

My head starts to hurt as the thoughts twist in my brain, playing over and over again. I've got to stop and think.

Emily won't let me get caught. She's going to help me.

I move from hole to hole, finding him looking in each room and closet, every hiding place.

I find Emily in her bedroom, packing a suitcase. She's in her underwear. The lovely outfit she had on tossed over the foot of the bed.

"Isaiah." Her sweet voice calls, as she turns towards the door.

So that's his name.

"Yeah?" He calls back. His voice floats up the attic stairs. Sweat rolls down my back. He must be at the door.

"Come here."

His footsteps falls farther away. He comes into view in her bedroom.

Why is he in your bedroom?

Of course, she's trying to help me. She knows I'm trapped. She's using the only distraction she can think of.

Even though I know what she's doing, as I watch her reach out and pull him close by his belt, it angers me. It's my fault that she's reduced to this. I wasn't careful enough. Now she's forced into this so I can get away.

"What are you doing? I was almost done." His voice floats through the ceiling.

"No one is here but us. Maxie would be barking." She watches his face. He follows her to the bed kissing her.

I can't condone her methods, but if he'd found me I don't know what might have happened. I can't have things between me and Emily disrupted. I watch them fall into the bed, him pulling off his shirt, pushing her legs wide, bending to kiss the inside of her thigh, and moving his hands up to her panties.

No one should be touching her. No one but me. He's going to pay for this, but I'll have to deal with that later. I have to get out of here. The sooner I'm gone, the sooner she can stop this charade. I hear her moan as I get up off the floor and tiptoe my way to the stairs.

Once out of the attic, I close the door silently. Unable to resist, I move down the hall and stand outside her bedroom door. My ears full of moans and heavy breathing.

I clench my fists at my sides, and peek around the corner of the door, careful to stay hidden.

She's naked from the waist down. He's between her legs with her hands tangled in his hair. Her groans tighten the front of my pants. My angry blood rushing to engorge me. He's going to pay for this, but I know she's thinking of me. We are in sync, Emily and me. She knew I needed help.

Before things go too far, I slip out the back door. I carefully replace the key in the potted plant, and jog across the backyard to where I parked my car one street over. I pull out my phone and dial.

"Hey, brother," my little sister's voice sighs in exasperation, "what is it now?"

"Who the fuck is Isaiah? And tell me why Emily is screwing him."

"I don't know. She won't take my calls."

I don't answer, I blow out a swear and hang up. Now I'll have to figure out who Isaiah is.

ISAIAH

I hold the key to my apartment in my outstretched palm. Emily stares at it as if it's going to bite her, and I laugh. "Take it. If you're staying here for a few days, you need to be able to come and go."

She picks it up and grabs her keys off the table by her front door. The locksmith just left, after changing out all her locks.

"Now, here are your new keys. Don't hide one like you did the last one. Give your spare to someone to hold for you in case you ever need it. Don't hide keys outside. Crooks know where to look."

She takes all three keys, smirking at me. "You sound like a cop."

I grin. "I am a cop, sweetie."

She laces my key and hers onto her key ring, and then hands me one. "Here, you can have the spare."

I take the key, trying not to make a production of the fact that we exchanged keys even though I'm jumping up and down inside like a stupid teenager. There's something about her that pulls me in, and I'm not about to try and fight it. I've never moved so fast with a woman before.

As I look down into her brown eyes and she smiles at me, there's a flutter in my chest. I've never imagined myself as the kind of guy who's scared of commitment, or the sort that runs from a good thing just because it feels too good. Hell, I've jumped into this with both feet and want more. I can't get enough of her, but I don't want to scare her away so I do my best to play things casual. I also want her to know that I'm here for her and that I'm hers now. I dubbed myself boyfriend this morning and she didn't fight it. I took that as a good sign.

"So, I've been thinking about what you told me. I think, for now, I'll make a record of the phone call that I had with him and do a harassment report. It will be a simple record that you told me that he was bothering you, and that I advised him to stop. The other stuff, we don't know for sure that's him, so let's leave that out for right now. If he bothers you again, you call the police, or call me. Got it?"

She glances down, nodding. "Yeah. I feel like I'm being a pain in the butt. I don't want to put you to work every time you're with me."

I crouch down so that I can meet her eyes, and she smiles at me. "You're not a pain in the butt. You are having a hard time, and I'm able to help you through it. One day you might need to be there for me through a hard time. That's what we do for each other. Don't feel that way, please."

"Ok. I'll try. This is all crazy, isn't it?" She looks up at me, uncertainty in her gaze.

"What is? All this weirdness?"

"Well that, and me and you. We kind of fit together."

As our eyes meet, I feel that flutter in my chest again. "We do fit together. It's easy when it feels right."

She bites her lip, and the uncertainty in her eyes drifts away. "Yeah, I guess so." Her voice is soft.

"You ready to head out?"

"I think so. Did you already put everything in the car?" She bends and clips a leash on her dog.

"Yep. Come on, let's drop her off, and I'll take you out for dinner."

A few hours later, her dog has made herself at home on a blanket that Emily laid out in the corner of the living room. She's sitting in my recliner, stretched out in pajama shorts and a matching, yellow, spaghetti strap tank top watching TV. For a moment, I stand in the hallway toweling off my hair just watching her.

She's going to want to go home in a few days, which is understandable. I can't deny, however, that seeing her here in my house like this makes me feel like this is where she belongs, with me.

I'm going to fall in love with her.

It's as clear as day. The moment I opened the door for her last night and saw her bright and smiling face, I knew it. When she made love to me on the couch, it was sealed. I'm hers and I'm not going to fight it.

Tossing the towel into the hamper, I step out of the bathroom in my pajama pants and stand behind the recliner, bending over her. She grins up at me.

"Mmm, you smell yummy."

I give her an upside down kiss, soft lips tempting mine, stealing my breath. "Thank you. You look yummy."

She giggles.

"You need anything, sweetheart?" I give her another soft kiss.

"No, I'm very content."

Looking down into her eyes, pouring myself into her, I sigh. "Can I keep you company then?"

"Yes, please."

I was going to sit on the couch, but the nearness of her is making me want to touch her. I crawl into the chair, straddle her hips, and lean over her. She smiles.

"I can't see the TV."

"I don't see the problem."

Her arms go around my neck and pull me down into her kiss. I love her reactions to my touch and my kiss, her soft sighs, and the way she tugs at my clothes when they seem to be in her way. As our kiss deepens and becomes more urgent, her hands slip into my pants and onto my ass making me grin.

"Want to go to bed?" I rub my nose to hers and search her eyes.

Her answer is almost a whisper, which catches my heart as if she reached in and grabbed it with her fist. "Okay."

I get up and pull her with me. The TV goes off, the door gets locked, and the lights get turned out.

She squeaks with delight when I pick her up and cup her perfect ass in my two big hands. Her legs go around my waist and her hands into my hair and she looks at me like I'm the only man in the world.

"I'm so damn glad you're here," I whisper.

She leans and kisses me. The taste of her mouth stirring up blood and enticing a groan from my chest. Before long she's tangled with me in a sensual knot and our clothes have found their way to the floor. I can't keep my lips off her body or my hands off her as she slides her hands up my back, welcoming me into her hips with tender eyes that are dark with sexual need.

Later, I watch her sleeping. This guy worries me. My gut tells me that there is more to this than just a crush. If he hurts her, I swear on everything I hold dear, I will make him pay.

CHAPTER 9

NOAH

I stand in my oversized shower as the showerheads spray overly hot water on me from every direction. All I can think about is who that man was with Emily yesterday. I tried to get into his car, but the door was locked and I was afraid that breaking the window would draw too much attention.

I've got to get a grip. I'm getting too reckless. I was almost caught yesterday. I'm not usually this way. I lather up for the fifth time, as is my ritual every morning and evening. I'd rather skip work and go see Emily today. She must be missing me. I can't do that, however. It's not how I became the success I am, and Emily would never approve. She would want to be proud of me. I have to be able to give her everything, and I can't do that if I stop working. She'd never respect a lazy man.

Perhaps, after our wedding, I can take her to Spain and retire with her in a villa. We can make love on the beach all day. I imagine her sun kissed skin and her red hair wet from the ocean. Her giggle plays in my mind as water pours over me. I ache in my belly for her as I imagine her biting that lip as I oil up her bare breasts in the afternoon sun on our private beach, and later holding her down and moving inside her. The love in her eyes... I can't wait to tell her everything I've planned.

As I dress in a charcoal suit, over a yellow shirt and tie, I think about the talk with the police officer when I called her. It's bothering me. *How did it happen to be that I called her just when she was with a cop? And why would she tell a police officer that I was bothering her when she loves me?* My attention isn't a bother. She welcomes it with the smiles she gives me and the sparkle in her lovely eyes. It confuses me. There must be some other reason.

Of course, the answer comes into my head and I laugh at myself, going over my suit with a lint roller. She's testing me. Of course she is. She can't tell me she loves me until I show her that I'm here no matter what. *And why wouldn't she want me to prove myself?* She's a gorgeous, young, smart woman. She's chosen me, and she knows what I want.

Peace settles over me. I can pass this test. I'll never give up on her.

At lunch time, I'm ushered into the Katy Police Department after a text to my friend, Detective Sergeant Julie Barton. After a call, I'm welcomed into the secure door and down the hall to her office, where I find her sitting behind her desk. She's talking to a tall, blond man. My heart thumps once against my ribs. I know the back of that head. He was with my Emily yesterday. The one she called Isaiah. He has a gun on his hip, and a police badge etched on the pocket of his polo shirt.

"Noah," Julie smiles warmly at me, standing up. "You made it. This is Detective Penrose. Penrose this is my friend Noah Burrell."

He turns his body, and I recognize the flash of recognition light in his eyes for a brief moment. His eyes travel over me as he sticks out his hand, offering it to me as if he has no idea who I am.

So, this is Isaiah. Isaiah Penrose.

I grasp his hand with a smile and a firm handshake with eye contact. I can almost feel him daring me to say something.

Of course, I just smile. This is part of Emily's test.

This is why he told me to stay away.

"Penrose, he owns Blue Liners, you know the place," Julie offers, smiling as she shuffles papers around on her outrageously cluttered desk.

Isaiah nods, shifting his weight. "For sure, I've been in there several times. You provide the police with a lot of support and do a lot for the community." He gives me a sideways look without a smile.

"Thank you. I try."

Julie opens and closes a drawer, drawing my attention back to her. She's pretty, middle-aged, and has chestnut hair pulled into a tight bunI try to overlook the clutter and mess in here. The piles of paper and the fact that there isn't an inch of her desk that isn't covered by something makes me want to toss a lit match in here.

"Noah and I are headed out for lunch, do you want to join us?" she chirps, pocketing keys.

"No, thanks. I'm meeting my girlfriend for lunch today." He moves for the door, looking me dead in the eyes for a brief moment as she passes me.

The bitter taste of bile rises in my throat to the back of my tongue. I swallow it back down. I ignore the remark as he exits the office, turning back to a smiling Julie.

"Where do you want to eat?" I smile as she walks around the desk.

EMILY

It's around lunchtime when my phone vibrates in the back pocket of my jeans. I smile as I pull my phone out because I'm expecting it to be Isaiah. I still can't believe how deliriously happy he's got me, despite all the strange goings-on I've been dealing with.

My smile vanishes. It's Caroline calling me. I don't even know how I feel about it, to be honest. I don't know for certain that she's done anything wrong, but I can't imagine why she would be acting like I forgot entire conversations, unless something really is wrong with me, or she is in cahoots with Noah for some reason. I've got no proof of anything, just bad feelings and strange goings-on. I ignore the call and shove my phone back into my pocket. Nothing solves a problem like refusing to face it, eh?

I guess I could confront her and tell her that I know what's going on, but what's the point? I'm not sure I'm even ready to face the truth.

Not long after, Le approaches me as she comes back into the pharmacy booth from her break. "Hey boss lady, there is someone outside asking for you."

My senses go on high alert, but I struggle not to let it show. "Who?"

She shrugs. "Some woman."

Okay, it's a woman. It's not Noah. I take a cleansing breath. It's probably a customer. "Thanks."

I head in the direction she points, and I find Caroline standing in the makeup section. I almost turn and walk away. Instead, I approach her and I motion for her to follow me outside as I pass.

"I've been worried sick. Why aren't you answering my calls?" she asks as the doors close automatically behind us.

I turn to face her. Biting back what I'd really like to say, I take a breath, remind myself to be halfway civil, and cross my arms. "Why, worried that I'm losing it?"

She gapes at me for a moment. "I didn't say that."

"So then please, go on." I tilt my head.

"I'm worried because you stopped answering. You don't call me anymore. I thought we were going to plan the wedding, but you've dropped off the face of the earth. Can't you at least tell me what I did?"

I glance around before my gaze settles on the pavement. "Caroline, I don't even know. I just can't right now."

Her face pales a bit. "What are you talking about?"

"You acted like I was nuts, and I don't understand it. You said I knew all this stuff when it was the first time I heard it. I had no idea that you are Noah's sister. I didn't even tell you that he'd been bothering me at work, I think that's a pretty heavy coincidence that you know him and suddenly this has been going on."

"What are you talking about? What do you mean? Are you accusing me of something?"

I take a deep breath. Of course she isn't going to admit to anything. "Someone has been breaking into my house. Your brother has been bothering me for months. How do I know you're not helping him somehow? How did he even know about me? He just showed up one day in the pharmacy and hasn't been out of my face since that day. Did you tell him about me? Did you let him into my house?" The words tumble out in a rush. Possibly unfair accusations, but maybe not.

"Emily, what is wrong with you? How can you accuse me of something like that? Are you crazy? Look, I'm sorry that someone is bothering you, but Noah is friends with the police chief, the commissioner for God's sake. You can't possibly imagine that he would... this is ridiculous and unfair... I—"

"No, what isn't fair is the fact that I've been run out of my own house because I might not be safe there. It's not fair that I don't know this man and he won't leave me alone..." My voice cracks as a lump forms in my throat. I try to swallow it. "That isn't fair. I've been reduced to hiding. And you're still feeding me lines. What if he wants to hurt me?"

Caroline narrows her eyes "He wouldn't hurt you. You have no idea what you are talking about."

Part of me knows it's true, but I don't know anything for sure. All I have are assumptions. Nothing concrete. Silence falls between us, I don't know what to say. Anger, fear, and confusion swirl inside me like a tornado, tying my tongue in the process. Our eyes meet, hers start to fill with water, and I look away, anywhere but into her face.

"I just think you should have a little more evidence before you start tossing around accusations like that. He's my brother. I know him. He's..." she fades out, shaking her head.

"You just don't know what's been going on."

"I know, you stopped talked to me."

Silence again. She speaks the truth. I swallow a lump forming in my own throat, threatening tears. She wipes her own tears from her cheeks.

"So, we will be in touch about the wedding, I guess?"

I shrug, not knowing what else to do. Without a word, Caroline walks away. Her heels click on the pavement as she heads to her car, wiping away tears.

I stand outside in the sunshine for a few minutes, willing the tornado inside me to calm. Turning towards a bench not far away to take a seat, I see Isaiah striding towards me on long legs. He is smiling under dark sunglasses as he crosses the parking lot. The sight of him, his blond hair shining in the sun, sets off butterflies in my stomach.

"Hey, baby." He grins.

My stomach curls and uncurls. "Hey."

"Can you get away for lunch now?" He lifts his glasses and puts them on his head, showing off his pretty eyes.

"Yes, I was just hoping that you would show up. Let me go inside and let them know."

A few minutes later, I'm settled into his front seat as we are pulling out of the parking lot.

"Was that Caroline's car?"

"Yes," I groan and give him the full story.

I give him my order as he pulls up to the drive-thru of the burger place. "I still don't have any answers. She swears that Noah wouldn't do something like this."

"Of course, she's his sister. Either she's lying, or its just one family member sticking up for another. You know how that goes."

I don't respond, and instead play the short exchange in my head again and again. Maybe she really didn't do anything wrong. Maybe it isn't him. Maybe... there are lots of maybes. Too many to swallow.

He pulls up to the drive-thru window and pays for the food. The car is suddenly filled with the scent of burgers and fries. I open one of the bags and start eating fries.

"Hey, woman, you want to share?"

With a smile, I feed him fries. His soft lips brush my fingertips, making me want to kiss him.

The fries are gone by the time we get to the park. He parks by a bench under a big maple tree.

After eating, I scoot over to him, our thighs touching. He turns his head giving me a slow smile that gives me goose bumps. Taking my hand, he laces his fingers with mine and presses his lips to the back of my hand.

"I want to say thanks." I look away from his smiling face and up to the tree.

"For what, all the mind blowing sex?"

I laugh, giving him a sideways grin. "No, for taking care of me and making me feel safe."

He leans close to my ear. "You're welcome. You don't think it's mind blowing?"

I turn my head and find his face so close to mine that I take in a sharp breath and forget to let it back out. "No, baby, it's nuclear."

My lips are caught in a kiss. After a moment, I can't stop myself from climbing into his lap, astraddle his thighs. He slides his hands up my thighs to my hips. I wrap my arms around his neck and sigh against his lips.

"We need to have more lunches like this." The words are mumbled against my throat. I giggle. This guy makes me happy. I forget the world when I'm with him. I forget things like guys that won't leave me alone.

"As much as I hate to spoil this, I need to let you know that I saw Noah at work before I left to come see you."

"What? Why? Why was he there?" My voice goes up an octave.

He tucks my hair behind my ear. The touch would normally sooth me, but I'm so surprised by what he's just told me that I blink instead of leaning into the warmth of his hand.

"He was having lunch with my Sergeant. I don't know how they know each other. She introduced him as her friend. I just happened to be in her office at the time. We'd just got back from a homicide scene."

I forget that he's a real life detective sometimes. Going on calls and looking at dead bodies, being the guy that saves the day after some awful tragedy when he locks up the bad guy. No wonder he sits here looking so calm. I'm panicked inside, and he's just gazing at me with copper colored eyes as if it's nothing.

My mind starts reeling. Everything that has happened over the last couple of weeks has faded into the background because this blond hottie I'm sitting on makes me feel human again. I forgot to be scared.

This problem is far from solved.

"Hey, take a breath," he whispers. "I'm not going to let anything happen to you, baby."

How can he be sure? Noah, whoever he is, whatever his problem is, found Isaiah. I'm sure it's only a matter of time before he finds me again. That is, if he was the one screwing around with me at home, and assuming that's even what was going on.

"Isaiah, what if he's dangerous?" My voice cracks.

His eyes go serious. "I'm dangerous, too. He better not fuck with someone I care about."

There is an edge to his voice that tells me he means it. He cares about me, already. I sigh. I care about him too, more than I expected possible at this juncture in our relationship.

"You care about me?"

His eyes soften. He touches my face. "I do. I won't let him hurt you."

I don't see how he can make this promise. "You aren't with me all the time. That's not something you can guarantee."

He nods, blowing out a breath. "Then just know that I'll do everything in my power to keep it from happening."

I stand up. He follows, pulling me into his arms. I bury my face in his chest and breathe in the scent of him.

"I believe you."

"Come on, let me get you back to work."

CHAPTER 10

NOAH

Lunch was uneventful, apart from never ending flirting that is. I guess old habits die hard. I got what I needed when she introduced me to this Penrose guy. It all worked out without me having to even ask her for anything.

As soon as I leave the restaurant, I dial my private detective's number and put him to work.

My palms start to sweat as I speed towards her house. I need to be near Emily; even if it's just her things, her dog, the scent of her on the pillow, or the feel of silky underthings slipping between my fingers.

I park two streets over this time. I try to keep from breaking into a run as I walk towards her house. I imagine how pleased she will be when she sees all the clothes that I've bought for her; the sexy under things and beautiful clothes in luxurious fabrics that will caress her perfect skin. Only the best for my angel.

The key is right where I left it, as it always is. I smile as I wipe the dirt off and put it in the lock. I'll have to water this plant. She seems to have forgotten it again. The key slides in roughly. I turn it, but nothing happens. No click. Furrowing my brow, I try again. The door won't open. That's when I notice it. Shiny new locks. Fuck. The key falls from my hand.

Going around the house, I try each door and each window. By the time I make it back to the back door, I'm shaking. She's locked me out. I can't get inside.

I can't catch her scent in the bed and be close to her. I can't check my camera's positions. I can't take care of her dog. Pushing my hands into my hair, I grab two fists full to keep from screaming. I'm so angry that my vision blurs and my head spins as my blood pressure rises.

I have to get inside.

Emily's been bad this time. This is going too far.

I cross the yard on swift legs, calling Julie.

JULIE MEETS me about a mile away from the CVS with a smile.

"You know, I can get your keys out of your car for you. I have a Slim Jim." She smiles as she shuts the door on her patrol car.

I laugh. "Hell no, I don't want you messing up something in my car with that thing. My girlfriend has keys. Just drive."

She shakes her head. "If you insist, come on."

A few minutes later, I pull my phone out of my pocket as she is pulling into the parking lot. "Shit!" I open up a text, or at least that's what I want it to look like. "I have to make a phone call. Do you mind running in? Her name is Emily. She's the pharmacist. Just tell her that her boyfriend locked his keys in his car and needs to borrow hers. That way I can get the spare." I doubt Emily would put it together that a cop can get into a car without keys. Like Julie, he'd likely just use a Slim Jim. It's a risk, but I'm desperate. I dial frantically.

Julie rolls her eyes at me. "I guess so. What's the big emergency?"

"May have lost a million-dollar deal. I have to deal with this. I need to get back to my office."

She nods and gets out as I dial.

When she comes out, I appear to be just hanging up. She plops down in the driver's seat, tossing the keys in my lap.

"She said don't forget to bring them back."

Well, that was easy. Thank God.

"Of course. Thank you!"

It doesn't take but a few minutes to get the keys copied. I'm able to sneak in and leave the keys with a cashier, telling him that I had to run.

I'll have no problems getting into her house now.

Now that this problem has been dealt with, I can deal with other things.

Emily has been bad. Time for her to be punished.

ISAIAH

Emily hasn't heard from Noah in over a week now. I can see the hope in her eyes when I look at her. She's thinking that it might be over. Nothing strange has happened. Caroline stopped calling. He isn't showing up at her work. I hope she's right, but in my gut I know that it never happens that way.

Twice in the last two days she's brought up going home. But both times she's looked at me and then dropped it. It's been almost two weeks with her here, playing house with me, and I'm addicted. I don't want her to go home. Forget this crazy guy. This is about me.

I want her to stay with me. I want to keep curling into her body at night. I want to walk by the bathroom and smile because I hear her singing in the shower. Seeing her in the kitchen, or playing with her dog, getting to know all those little things about a person that you only see when you are living with them. I don't want to lose that.

It's insane, I know this. No one has to tell me. I'm losing it for her, and I'm aching inside when I think of her packing up and going back home, splitting whatever this is up for a slower relationship. Screw slow. I want her, all of her, now.

With a groan, I try to think about something else as I walk down the hall. I hear the shower turn on and smile. The distinct sound of the shower door closing. I open the bathroom door. It's already starting to steam up. She wipes fog off the shower door and sees me just as I pull off my shirt.

Her teeth sink into her lip, making me smile.

I watch her watching me through the glass as I open my pants, strip down, and kick my clothes aside. She opens the shower door and invites me in.

Water drips over her naked body. She draws my eyes to her as she turns. She looks up at me with eyes that are growing darker with want.

"Hi." Her voice is breathy.

"Hi." I smile back, reaching behind her for the shampoo.

I motion for her to turn around and she grins at me as I fill my hand with fragrant shampoo and work it slowly into her hair. I massage her head with my fingertips, drawing a pleasant sigh as I caress her head. Her foamy hair slips in and out of my fingers. Slipping my lubed-up fingers down her neck, she moves into the touch.

"Turn," I order.

She does. Arching her back to rinse her hair out, she watches me with bedroom eyes as I reach for the conditioner. Her bare breasts brush my chest, sending want that makes my blood thick into my veins.

"I want you to stay until this is over."

For a moment she watches my face, and then turns to let me condition her hair.

"I can't stay here forever."

I slide my hands over her bare shoulders and down her arms. She takes in a breath as I move to the curve of her breasts, lingering slowly.

"I know, but I'm not sure this is over."

I stop touching her just long enough to put body wash into my palms. I slip my hands over her breasts, stomach, arms, and back. I touch her ass, moving around her hips. She turns to face me as I crouch to lather up her thighs.

She watches me with parted lips as I slip my hand between her legs. Her head falls back as I touch her slowly and deliberately.

"Stay with me." I ask roughly as I stand, still moving my fingers.

"It's not fair for you to ask when you're doing that," she pants.

I smile, gently pushing her against the wall. "You're beautiful when you're turned on."

She grips my shoulders, gasping.

I lean in, whispering in her ear. "Baby, tell me you'll stay."

God I want her. I drag my parted lips over her shoulder, tasting the heat of the water coming off her skin while her hands move over my body.

"Isaiah." My name comes out as a whimper as I nip at her neck and her ear. I shift positions so that I can hold her where I need her to push inside her.

She watches me love her with eyes half open, but emotions lingering as if they were wide. Our wet bodies slide easily. I growl her name and bite her lips gently as she clutches at my arms and back. Each movement pushes us closer and closer towards the precipice.

As steam swirls around us, and hot water pours into my face, I make rapid love to her against the stone wall of the shower. Her groans and breathy pleads pushing me faster and deeper into her.

She's making me fall in love with her.

Her nails grip me as she tightens around me. I know the feeling, the look, and the change in her breath. She's looking at me with a face that's a mask of the pleasure that explodes gloriously around her, around us both. Watching her, feeling her, makes me fall right along with her, and it's perfect.

She turns off the water. I don't move. Nuzzling her, I stare into her brown eyes letting my heart feel every bit of it, of her, of this moment with her. She looks right back at me, brushing soft lips against mine.

"Emily." I mutter against her perfect mouth. "Don't go."

Her hands on my face cause me to open my eyes.

"I'll stay until it's safe."

Peace crashes into me like a tsunami. "Thank you."

"Isaiah, is this about him... or about..."

I smile, for a brief moment wondering what to say. "Both. I want you safe. But frankly, this place feels like home now that you're in it."

Her eyes light up. "I know what you mean."

I hand her a towel and grab one for myself. "You want some coffee before bed?"

She smiles, bending to dry off. "Sure, thank you."

Without another word, I wrap the towel around my hips and leave the bathroom for the kitchen.

EMILY

"I need to go get some things from my house." I call as I shove my clothes into the washing machine.

I didn't bring that much with me. I was expecting to go home after a couple of days. Isaiah walks up to me with Maxie on his heels. "You want me to go with you? Are you sure you don't want me to pack up? We can stay at your house for a couple of days."

I chew on my lip as I close the lid and turn on the machine. "I guess we can, but let me go clean first. It's probably a mess."

He grins at me. "I'll come with you. I can help you."

I wince. "You don't understand. I'm a slob. I've been trying to be neat here, but..."

With a chuckle, he pulls me into his arms. "Woman, it's fine. A little mess won't run me off. Give me time to pack up and we'll head over."

He plants a light kiss on my lips, and he pops me on the butt with a laugh as he walks off.

As I unlock my front door, I already feel a little better. Isaiah stands behind me with our bags. Maxie is busy wrapping her leash around my legs as she dances, eager to be home.

When I step inside, the peaceful feeling vanishes. My chest heaves as a whimper bubbles up in my throat. "Fuck."

"What's wrong?" Isaiah steps in behind me. "Holy shit."

The walls are scrawled with the words *Bad Girl* in red paint. It's written dozens of times.

My couch has been ripped to shreds. Someone took a knife to it and destroyed it, along with the matching chair. Stuffing is everywhere. Broken glass crunches under my feet as tears blur my vision.

"Holy God, Isaiah—"

He shoves me out the front door, pulling his gun from his bag. His phone is already on his ear. "Emily, get outside. Hey, dispatch, I need a unit to 4333 Auburn Run..."

His voice fades as I pull Maxie outside. Sitting on the front steps, I collapse into tears.

While the police check my house, I call ADT and make arrangements to have an alarm installed.

I hear steps fall on my porch and a manly whisper hits my ears, "Hey."

The patrol officers just left. Isaiah sits beside me. He wraps an arm around my shoulder and plants a kiss on my ear.

"Is it the whole house, or just the living room?" My voice breaks. I turn, looking into his face.

"It's a mess, baby. I'm not going to lie. We don't know how he got inside. There's no signs of break in. Does anyone else have a key? Did you hide one somewhere?"

I shake my head. "No, just you."

"We didn't find any evidence that it was him. And we aren't staying here."

I stand up. "I guess I might as well get this over with."

Isaiah takes my hand, halting me with a tug. He cups my chin and tilts my face up forcing my eyes to his. "Just remember what's important, ok? There's a lot of damage, but you are ok. We can replace these things, but I can't replace you. You're amazing and strong and we will get through this." He brushes stray tears off my cheeks with his thumb.

"Why would someone do this?"

"I don't know, but I promise you, I'll find out everything I can."

He holds my eyes with his for a moment, and then we walk inside. In the kitchen, all my dishes are broken. I have to hold Maxie to keep her from walking in the glass. Isaiah takes her from me as I push through the front of the house and down the hall.

I feel his hands on my shoulders in the doorway of my bedroom. *Bad Girl* is scrawled on the walls here too. My mattress has been slashed, and the mirror over my dresser is broken. Those ugly words are written in paint across my headboard.

My clothes are in the bathtub with bleach poured over most of them. I need to get this cleaned up, but I can't make myself move. Isaiah pulls me into his chest and wraps me in his arms. I fall into heaving sobs against his chest. His hands run up and down my back, and his whispers touch my ears as I cry against him. "I'm so sorry."

Mattress, clothes, broken furniture all go in the trash. The broken glass is cleaned up, and the painters are hired for the walls. As the house gets emptier and emptier, the ugly words on the wall seem to scream at me louder and louder, and I can't help but wonder if I did something to make this guy think that... I don't know what he thinks. I didn't mean to lead him on, or send any signals, is this partly my fault? The idea turns my stomach as I watch Isaiah load our bags back into his car, ready to go back to his apartment.

CHAPTER 11

ISAIAH

I was calm. I was there for her. The big strong man, but inside I was a raging mess. Angry isn't the word.

Murderous is more accurate.

Flying into a rage isn't what she needs. So instead I swallow it all. I take her back to my apartment where she flops down on the couch, defeat all over her face. The light gone from her eyes.

Falling to my knees, I rest between her legs, my head in her lap and my arms around her waist. Her hands move into my hair.

I hate seeing her this way—crying, upset, sad. When she is happy it makes me feel like everything in my life is perfect.

I'm falling in love with her.

She'd probably tell me I'm crazy. It's only been a couple of weeks. But hell, when it's right, it's right. I feel like she's a force of nature, like thunder.

I sit up and move in close to her face. As her eyes search mine, my heartbeat picks up. "I want to have sex with you in the bathtub." I mutter close to her lips.

She smiles. "Sex is your answer for everything."

"Is that a bad thing?"

She laughs. "No, it's my answer for everything too."

I touch her lips with mine. "This is why we are perfect for each other."

She follows me to the bathroom where I start the water and add some soap for bubbles in the garden bathtub.

She leans on the counter watching me. "How did you ever find an apartment with a bathroom like this? It's glorious."

As the tub fills, I move to her and grasp the hem of her shirt. She gives me a crooked smile and lifts her arms so I can pull her t-shirt off. She returns the favor and tosses my shirt aside.

I run my fingers through her hair, and her brown eyes soften. "I'm completely crazy about you."

She bites her lip, running her hands over my chest. "Well, you're half right."

I laugh. She unbuckles my pants. My heart slams against my ribcage when her fingers brush my stomach. Leaning over, I kiss her. She responds with a slow eagerness that makes my blood rush in my ears. The feel of her tongue curling around mine as we finish stripping each other down is enough to make me forget my own name.

When we are laughing together and water is splashing out of the tub, I look up into her eyes as she straddles my hips and I know that I love her. I have no doubt and no fear. I think I have since that moment in the coffee shop when she spilled her coffee on me. It's why I was so heartbroken when she ran from me.

But we found each other again. When I'm with her and she's touching me, looking at me like I'm the only thing she can see, I forget everything else.

"You belong to me." She smiles down at me.

I grip her hips. "Every part of me, baby." My words come out raspy as she shifts.

Good God, I love this woman.

I STARE DOWN at the address scrawled across the notepad sitting on my desk, telling myself that I need to stay away.

16841 Gates Creek.

I pocket my keys. I don't need to go. I need to stay here and work on the other cases that I have piled on my desk. I need to return the list of phone calls from citizens asking for follow-up information on their cases.

I walk out the door leaving the files and messages behind. I slip my phone into my pocket and my sunglasses onto my head.

I'm going.

Of course, when I get to the address there is a big gate around the property. I pull up, hit the button on a box, and a voice comes across asking me who I am.

"Detective Penrose, Katy Police."

There is a moment of silence, and then the gate opens. I pull into a long paved driveway. Cypress trees line either side as I drive up. Finally, I reach the front of a huge house.

Business must be good.

When I get to the door, it opens before I can push the buzzer. I was expecting his help to answer the door, since people like this don't seem to ever have the time to open their own front doors.

I'm greeted by the unsmiling face of Noah Burrell. His black eyes greet me with a smugness that makes me want to laugh in his face. His black hair and tanned skin makes his yellow golf shirt pop.

"Detective."

"I need to have a few words with you. May I come inside?"

He steps aside. I step in. The house smells of antiseptic and looks unbelievably clean. The sound of my shoes clicking across the black and white floor echoes in the big room. He leads me to a sitting area where everything is white: the couches, chairs, and the shaggy carpet.

"Can I offer you something?"

He sits across from me, spreading his arms across the back of the loveseat. I meet his eyes.

I want to hurt him.

"No. I'm here to tell you that I know it was you that got into Emily's house and destroyed it. I don't know what you think you're doing, but you need to stay away."

Noah leans forward, clasping his hands and resting his elbows on his knees. "Are you here to charge me with a crime?"

"No, I'm not here officially."

He glares at me with hate in his freaky eyes. *Who the hell has black eyes anyway? Are they real or is he trying to freak people out with some funky brand of contacts?*

"Then I think you best watch what you say."

"I'll get to the bottom of this. Have no doubt. Back the hell off, Burrell."

He smiles at me. It's a cocky, *fuck you* of a smile. "You have no idea, Detective."

"Then why don't you enlighten me?"

He laughs, standing up and stepping closer to me as if he's daring me to stand up. I rise slowly. We are eye to eye. I have to tell myself to breathe. I remind myself not to put my hands on him.

"I don't owe you a thing. I don't appreciate you coming here making accusations."

I take a step. We are almost nose to nose. His breath smells like coffee.

"I'm telling you, if you fuck with her again, if you come near her, if you even fucking say her name, I'll come back and make you sorry that you ever did."

His eyebrows go up and he smiles. "I'll remember that next time I speak with your Sergeant."

"As long as you remember."

We stare each other down for a moment before I turn and walk out the door.

Time to go see Caroline now.

The drive downtown into Houston takes me forty minutes. I spend half of that talking on the phone to Emily, but I don't tell her what I'm doing. I don't know what she would say. I don't want to be talked out of this.

Caroline is the manager of the Southeast Texas region of Noah's company. The office is on the ninth floor in a high rise downtown. I step off the elevator and into an office directly across the hall. A perky blonde sits behind a desk. Her eyes drift over me before she smiles and asks to help me.

"I need to see Caroline Brown."

"Do you have an appointment?"

I pull out my badge. "Tell her Detective Penrose needs to see her."

Her smile flickers, and she picks up the phone.

Fifteen minutes later, I'm sitting in Caroline's office with a cup of coffee is in my hand. Caroline eyes me, shifting and fidgeting just enough to tell me that she's nervous.

A picture of her and her fiancé, my college buddy, sits on her desk.

"What's up, Isaiah?"

"Emily told me that you came to see her the other day, and that you two had an argument."

She crosses her arms defensively. "I don't see what that has to do with the police. It's just a disagreement between friends."

"I don't know how much you two have talked since your engagement party, but she and I are dating. And I think you might already know, but your boss or brother or whatever his is, is causing her some problems."

She glances around the room and picks up a pen and starts to fiddle with it.

"Well, I'm happy for you two. I still don't—"

"Don't lie to me, Caroline. Something is going on. Emily doesn't want to see it, but I can see it. Be straight with me."

The color drains from her face. "I don't know what you mean."

"You think I can't find out? Let me tell you something, Caroline. Noah is stalking Emily. I think he is dangerous. I'm concerned for her safety."

She blinks at me. "My brother wouldn't do that. I think you need to leave."

"I don't know what he's capable of. Let me show you something."

I pull up the pictures I took of Emily's house on my phone and lean on the desk.

Her mouth falls open and a soft sound like a squeak comes out of her as I flip through the pictures. "Oh God. Who did this?"

"I can't prove it, but I suspect he did. Now, you look at this and tell me that we are dealing with a stable man. I want the truth, and I want it now. Tell me what happened."

I put my phone back in my pocket, and I sit back in the leather chair. She watches me, breathing funny for a moment.

"You have no right to come in here demanding answers with no proof of anything. Take your assumptions and get out, and don't come back without a warrant." She stands up and walks to the door. With stones set in her eyes, she holds it open for me, daring me with her gaze to do anything but walk out.

Knowing my ass is on the line if she calls my boss, I force my pride down my throat and rise from the chair. "I am not finished with this."

"Good. Do your job and find out who actually did it instead of accusing innocent people."

I start to walk out the door, but then hesitate at the last minute, and make one last effort to reach her before I go. "If you don't tell me something very bad might happen. I need you to be honest with me, Caroline. This is off the record. I'm not here in any official capacity."

"He won't... he wouldn't hurt her. He loves her. He'd die before he let anything happen to her."

My heart stops beating. This is what I was afraid of, but I convinced myself that it would be something else. I lean forward, placing my elbows on her desk.

"How can he love her? He doesn't even know her." My voice is low, but harsh.

"They talk all the time. He sees her every day. You don't have a clue, detective. You've only known her a few weeks. He's known her for months." The words come out strong, certain. She has no doubt in what she's saying, that much is clear.

"There is something wrong with him, Caroline. How could you

believe that making her think she was crazy would be anything other than hurtful to her? Did you let him into her house?"

She shakes her head. "Get out."

"If anything happens to her, you are partly responsible."

I stand up. She balks at me, unmoving as I walk out the door. It closes with a slam behind me.

NOAH

"Tell me what you found out." I stare across my desk at Able, my private investigator.

He tosses a file across my desk. "Not much really. I followed him and dug around all week long and didn't come up with much."

I pick up the file and open it, skimming the report as he continues.

"He's a good cop, doesn't get into trouble. He got out of college and went straight into the police academy, graduated top of his class. He's been working at Katy PD since he was twenty-two. He's thirty-one, never married, no kids. His dad lives in Galveston. He has a sister, a niece, and a nephew. He's clean. There is a woman living with him; she's been there all week, but she isn't on the lease."

I look up at him. "What's her name?"

"Emily something. She's a pretty, little redhead. Her name is in there." He nods towards the file.

So, that's where she went. I stare down at his address. A luxury apartment complex in the Woodlands. "How does he afford this apartment on a cop's salary?"

Able shifts his large body in the seat. The leather groans under him. "He has some money from his mom's life insurance. Looks like she named him and his sister the beneficiaries of her account when she got sick. He makes decent money."

"What kind of hours does he keep?" I close the file.

"Monday through Friday, except when he's on call. I couldn't get that schedule. The cops are tight with that crap and won't release it. He works banker's hours mostly, now that he's not on patrol anymore. He's been a detective for about a year."

I nod, pulling my checkbook out of the drawer. Able's eyes light up, although he tries not to let it show.

"Thank you, Able, you have been very helpful."

"No problem. What did this guy do anyway?"

I smile. "Nothing. Just looking into hiring him for security. Can't be too careful. People lie on resumes all the time."

He nods as I scratch out the check. I pay him twice what I offered to pay him a week ago when I hired him. With a rip, I tear the check out and hand it to him.

His eyes widen, and I lean back in my chair with a smile.

"I appreciate your time. I'm sure I'll call you again in the future, if anything else comes up."

He rises, pocketing the check and shoving his hand out for me to shake. I swallow, grasping his hand and enduring his enthusiastic gratitude. As soon as he closes the door, I pump hand sanitizer into my hand and get up, headed for the bathroom to wash my hands. I hate touching strangers. It makes me sick. I turn the water up as hot as I can stand it and lather my hands over and over again, until my skin is pink and burning.

So, Emily isn't staying at home. She's with lover boy. I glance at my watch. It's just past lunch. If he is right, Isaiah and Emily won't be home.

Time to pay a visit.

I find the apartment with no problem. Neither of their cars are here. I double check the report just to make sure before I pull my keys out.

Time to see if he gave her a key.

After trying four keys, the lock clicks and I hear Maxie barking as

I push the door carefully open. The place is clean, except for a little bit of clutter. Of course, with Emily staying here I suppose that's to be expected. I'll have to break her of these bad habits.

Crouching, I scratch the dog's head. She licks my fingers, and I scold her, moving to the kitchen to wash my hands.

The far wall is one massive window that is covered with vertical blinds. It really is a lovely apartment. Seems Detective Penrose has good taste.

Unable to locate a security system, I decide that there must not be one and I move freely around the apartment. I find Emily's clothes and deeply breathe in the scent of her body.

God I've missed her.

I haven't been able to see her in days. Now that she's afraid and her detective boyfriend is around, I've been forced to keep my distance. I can't stay upset with her, knowing that she's just biding her time with him. She's waiting for me to come and get her, and for me to pass her test.

"We will be together soon, my love." I mutter. Laying on the bed, I stick my face in one of the pillows smelling her perfume and shampoo.

There must be a place to hide in here. I look through closets and under the bed. It's all too risky. I suck air through my teeth and run a hand over my head.

I suppose I'll have to watch the place and catch her home alone. Maybe he will get called out in the middle of the night and I can catch her sleeping.

I look down. Maxie sits happily at me feet. "Did you miss me, girl?" I bend and pat her head. "Don't worry, I won't stay gone long this time."

Soon. It won't be long now. I'll win her heart and she will be my good girl.

I hope that she doesn't force me to punish her again.

CHAPTER 12

EMILY

I've been struggling with temptation for days. Today I break down. I glance around as I type Noah's name into the computer. No one is paying attention. It's not like looking at a customer's file is out of bounds for my job. I need to calm down.

Maybe something in here will give me a clue as to what's going on in his head. His name comes up and I select it. A rock hardens in my stomach as I stare at the screen at a list of anti-psychotics, anti-depressants, and medications commonly used to treat OCD. But nothing that has recently been filled.

Well isn't this lovely.

Chewing on my lip, I wonder if knowing this would help Isaiah. I know he's been looking into things for me, but if I get caught releasing this information I could lose my license. I scroll further. I find personal information and his doctor's name. I scribble down the number for his cell and his doctor. I scroll further looking for family, but there is no information listed there. He didn't list Caroline as next of kin, odd.

Maybe he needs help. *With this kind of history, isn't it possible that he doesn't know what he's doing?* Maybe he needs someone to call his doctor or tell him that he needs help.

I swallow, fingering the paper in my pocket as I exit out of the file. He's got mental health problems. His mind is diseased and he very likely can't help it. I suppose I shouldn't be feeling sorry for him, but I do. What if I could try to explain things to him? He might see reason. He has to have control of part of his mental facilities; he runs a multi-million-dollar business.

Besides, every time he sees me he's so nice. I don't think he's really going to hurt me. Maybe he's confused. He can't possibly realize that what he's doing is scaring me. With this history, he likely is not in his right mind.

I can almost see Isaiah's face if I told him that we should sit down with Noah and talk to him. I don't know if Noah is dangerous, but the fact that this may very well be something he can't control makes me feel bad for him.

Maybe I could call him.

I can explain to him that he's hurting me and tell him that I know he doesn't mean too. Maybe he can understand that.

The clock on the screen reads three fifteen. I take a deep breath and tell Le that I'm stepping out for a moment. My hands are shaking as I pull my phone out of my pocket.

Do I dare? I'm not the scaredy cat type. I take things as they come to me. I'm not used to handling someone with a mental illness, but it can't be that much different than handling someone that is normal, can it? He seems pretty normal other than this mess.

I type his number off of the paper I have in my pocket into my phone as I walk outside, sitting down on the bench. He's always nice to me when he comes up here to talk to me, so a phone call isn't really dangerous, right?

It can't hurt to try.

NOAH

As I drive back to my office, my phone starts to ring in the cup holder beside me. With a groan, I glance over at the screen prepared to ignore whoever it is. I almost veer off the road when I see who's calling me.

Emily. My Emily is calling me.

Holding my breath, I pick up the phone and press it to my ear as I pull over, my tires flinging gravel from the shoulder of the road. "Hello?"

"Hi, um... is this Noah?"

I close my eyes at the sound of her sweet voice saying my name. God I've dreamed of this moment. I take a slow deep breath. "Yes, Emily?"

She breathes heavily into the phone for a moment. I anticipate the sound of her voice with a thundering heart.

"Noah, can we talk for a moment? I'm sure you're very busy, but I think there are some things that need to be said."

"Yes, of course. I'll always have time for you, Emily. You can say anything you need to say to me."

"Thanks. Look, I don't know how to say this to you, but... um... I know it was you that tore up my house. I realize that maybe you don't realize what you are doing, but it's hurting me. I don't like it and I want you to stop. I know you want us to be friends, don't you?"

"Yes. I want us to be friends, Emily. I know that you do too."

She breathes again. I close my eyes at the sound of her pant in my ear.

"I can't be friends with you if you are going to scare me."

"I will take care of you Emily. I'll pay for everything. I have so much I want to tell you. I'm so glad that you called me. You don't have to hide anymore or pretend."

"Noah, you don't have to do that. Just promise me that you won't scare me anymore. Please? I think maybe you need to go see your doctor. I think it will make you feel better."

Scare her? I guess my punishment frightened her. I'll have to make it up to her. She called me. Now I know we are meant to be together forever. If only I could just touch her.

"I didn't mean to scare you, Emily. I love you. I—"

"You love me?" Her voice is quiet.

It felt so good to say it out loud to her. I can't even think straight now. "Yes. I don't want to scare you, or hurt you."

She doesn't say anything for a long moment. She must be overwhelmed.

"Thank you. Just remember that we can't be friends if you are frightening me, okay?" Her voice is so damn sweet.

God I don't want her to hang up. I want to sit here and let her words curl around me, imagining she is here with me.

"Thank you for calling me, Emily. I appreciate you taking the time to talk to me about this. I'll make this up to you, okay? I promise."

"You don't need to do that. I need to go, so... bye, Noah."

"Bye, Emily."

I sit on the side of the road, my body electrified after hearing her voice say my name so intimately. I have to do something to tell her I love her now, so she won't be afraid of me.

I throw the car into gear, peeling out as I pull back onto the highway. I was starting to doubt myself, but now I know she loves me. She just needs me to prove my love to her before she can open up to me.

EMILY

After hanging up, I *stare down at my phone. I'm not sure what just happened. He loves me? How can he love me? He doesn't even know me? Will he listen? Should I have flat out told him to leave me alone?*

He seemed nice and didn't get angry with me or anything. I guess trying the gentle approach to start is okay. I should probably tell Isaiah what happened, just in case.

Oh, I hope he doesn't get mad at me. Maybe I should plan a nice dinner or something. And sex, the man likes sex.

Hell, I like sex, a lot, with him. My stomach curls up thinking about him. I wish so much that I had stayed with him the first time I met him. I feel like I wasted all these months away from him. I can only imagine the amazing place we might be in our relationship if I hadn't done such a stupid thing. Suddenly, thinking about him makes me want to hear his voice. Before I stand up to go inside, I dial his number.

I feel like I've known him for ages. It doesn't feel like we just met. We just clicked and became this instant couple. I don't know why I was so scared before. I love it.

"Hey, baby." His voice is a purr.

My stomach somersaults. "Hi. I just wanted to hear your voice."

"Missing me?" There is a smile in his words.

"Yes. I was thinking about how stupid I was that first night."

"Ah, yeah. I can't say I disagree with you. Making me miss you for all those months."

I laugh. "Did you? Think about me?"

"Yeah, more than I care to admit."

I bite my lip. He really does like me. Warmth spreads across my chest. I can't wait to see him. "I'm sorry. I shouldn't have left. Can you forgive me?"

He laughs lightly and it's like music to my ears. It soothes this hurricane that's rolling around inside my brain after talking to Noah.

"Honey, we're good. I can't stop smiling. You make me so damn happy."

"Really?"

"Really. I can't stop thinking about you, and I see you all the time."

The softness of his tone stirs the rhythm of my heart. "Isaiah, I really like you too, a lot." I like him more than a lot, way more.

"Say my name again," he whispers.

I take in a sharp breath and close my eyes. "Isaiah."

"I'll never get tired of that."

"Can I cook you dinner tonight?"

"I'd love that. I'll bring a bottle of wine."

"Okay. I need to get back inside. I'll see you then."

"Bye, Emily."

"Bye."

When I hang up, I'm all warm and fuzzy inside. As I stand, I'm grinning ear to ear. I feel like a high school girl again. He has this amazing power to calm the storm.

When Isaiah walks in I'm chopping veggies for a salad. The steaks are sitting on the counter and potatoes have been roasting in the oven. With a smile, he walks into the kitchen and sets a bottle of wine on the counter. He then traps me against the counter, his front pressed against my back.

"Look at you, being domestic," he whispers close to my ear.

I grin as a chill rolls down my spine. "Well, I thought because you are so cute maybe I could do something nice for you."

His lips are on my neck. "Hmm, she thinks I'm cute."

"So cute." I giggle.

"I got you something. That's why I'm late."

He dangles a gold chain in front of me. On the end of it is a breathtaking water lily with an opal in the center. As I reach up, he moves faster than me and fastens it around my neck.

"Isaiah! Oh it's lovely. You—"

"Didn't have to? I know. I wanted to. Like it?"

I look down, fingering the delicate flower before I turn to face him. His eyes are bright, smiling.

"I love it. I won't take it off. Thank you."

Leaning in, he kisses me. "You're welcome, angel."

His kiss is soft and makes me sigh. I'm getting used to being here with him every day. As he holds my face, giving me a kiss hello that would melt my fillings, I realize that the longer I stay, the harder it's going to be to leave when this is over. I'll cross that bridge when I get to it. He grins against my lips.

"Can I help you cook?"

"No. You can open this wine and watch me make these steaks."

He backs up and eyes me seductively as he unbuckles his gun belt.

"Yes ma'am."

Over dinner, I dread bringing up what I know I need to tell him, so I wait. After dinner, he pushes me against the wall in the hallway, looking down into my eyes. I grip his shirt in both fists, unable to find words for how I feel as I watch his face.

"I don't think I'll ever get enough of you," he whispers.

"I really hope you never do."

"It won't ever happen. You're so beautiful, Emily." He watches my eyes for a moment and touches my hair. "Have you ever been in love?"

The question catches me off guard. I haven't, not once. I was starting to wonder if I ever would feel that something for someone. "No, not until..." I catch myself about to blurt out what I haven't even admitted to myself yet.

He smiles, a slight knowing sort of smile as he gazes at my lips, and then back to my eyes.

"Not until what? Do you believe in love at first sight?"

My pulse picks up. "I don't know."

His smile reaches his copper eyes. "I never did, but I swear..." He takes in a deep breath. His chest heaves as he blows out the breath. "I believe in it now."

I didn't realize I was holding my breath until his next words come out a moment later. "It's okay, just breathe." His words are soft and wrap around my heart so tight it makes it stop beating.

I touch the buttons on his shirt. "Are you—?"

"Falling in love? Yes."

Oh God, he loves me. Damn if I don't love him too. I wait for my heart to start beating again before I say, "Me too."

He grins at me. "No kidding?"

I nod. He kisses me, finally. I'm pressed into the wall as he moans into my mouth, his tongue searching for mine. His hands find my hips, slip around to my ass, and push me into him. A whimper escapes me as fresh heat surges through my body, which is awakened by everything that is Isaiah. His scent and taste. The hard muscle of his chest and firm grip of his large hands. The way he breathes and groans when I kiss him.

Once in the bed, he holds my hands above my head, straddling me and pushing me into the mattress under his weight.

"Isaiah, say it for me," I say, when he pulls his mouth off mine and presses it into my throat.

He looks down at me. "I love you."

I take in a breath as he releases his grip on my arms so he can bend and press his mouth to my bare stomach. Dragging kisses across my belly, stirring up heat in the center of me, his voice echoes in my mind. He loves me.

"Isaiah." I whisper his name.

His head pops up.

"I love you back."

Our eyes lock together. He smiles, and then crashes into me with a groan. What's left of our clothes are ripped away in a sudden desperate desire for skin to skin contact. Every part of me wants to feel every part of him.

Soon I'm left gasping at hot, wet kisses inside my thighs. Later he's groaning when I invite him in with widespread legs. I pull his lips back to mine with a *please* moaned on my lips.

Tangled together, Isaiah pants as he rests his head on my chest. My skin still buzzes from his touch. I run my hand through his blond hair, pushing damp strands off his face.

"I love it when you do that," he mumbles.

"What, play with your hair?"

"Mmm hmm."

The heat coming off his body is scorching, but I don't want him to move. I know that I need to tell him about the phone call, but I don't want to ruin the moment by mentioning Noah.

I'd much rather revel in the feeling of Isaiah nuzzled into my body. I'll tell him tomorrow.

CHAPTER 13

ISAIAH

Rolling up on my elbow, I tug the blanket up to my hips. Emily does likewise, covering her chest. I lace my fingers with hers and swallow. Time to tell her what happened today. She loves me and I want to keep it that way. I want to keep everything out in the open. As much as I hate to ruin the moment, I need to be honest.

"I need to tell you something." My voice booms in the too-quiet room.

She wiggles under the blankets, her thigh brushing mine. "So, tell me."

"Don't be mad at me, but I went to see Noah today. Caroline too."

Her eyes widen slightly. "What? You did? I didn't know you were going to do that."

I nod, tracing her fingers with mine. "I went to his house and told him to stay away from you."

She sits up and the blankets fall, exposing her chest to me. I'm so distracted by the fullness of the curve of her body that I almost don't hear what she says next.

"Isaiah, did you threaten him? Will you get into trouble?"

Forcing my gaze up, I look into worried eyes. "I told him if he messed with you I'd make him sorry. He might tell my Sergeant. I'll deal with it if he does."

She stares at me, stone faced. "And Caroline?"

"I had a talk with her. I didn't get a lot out of her. She said he told her that he was in love with you. She was vague. I told her that if I find out she's involved and something happens to you I'd charge her with a crime. She kicked me out of her office."

"You did that for me?"

I nod. "Yes."

Emily leans in and kisses me. "Thank you. I need to tell you something, too." She lays down, chewing on her lip.

I wait in silence while her eyes move from me to the ceiling. "If I tell you, you can't mention it to anyone. I might lose my job."

"Of course."

"I pulled his file at work. He's been on a bunch of anti-psychotic and anti-depressants. I got to thinking maybe he can't help it. I thought maybe if I talked to him I could make him understand."

I bolt up. "What? What did you do?"

"I called him." Her face wrinkles when she sees the alarm in me. "I told him that I know it's him, and I know that he doesn't mean to scare me, and that I need him to stop. I said we can't be friends anymore if he's acting this way."

My heart rate picks up as what she says hits my ears. "Emily—"

She sits up, putting her hands on my shoulders. "Isaiah, he was nice. He told me that he didn't want to scare me and he wants to make it up to me. I told him not to. He told me that he loves me. That was it. He wasn't mean to me."

I take her face in my hands. "You don't understand. You can't give these people any attention. It feeds their delusion."

Her eyes tear. "I thought—"

"I know. You thought you could be sweet and ask him nicely and he would get it. He's sick, baby. He won't get it. The more you talk to him, the more it feeds him. He thinks he loves you. Hell, he might think you love him too. I'm no doctor, but I've dealt with enough mentally ill people to have a good idea about things. You have to ignore him. No matter what. You can't talk to him. No accepting gifts. No contact at all."

Tears slip from her eyes and over my fingers. I hate that she's crying, but she has to know and she's got to understand that he's not harmless.

"What if he shows up at my work?"

"Ignore him. Walk past him. Get someone to walk you to your car."

She nods, sniffing. "And gifts?"

"Send them back."

"I'll try. Won't he get mad?"

"Maybe. There's more than one way this can end. I don't much care if he gets mad. Promise me that no matter what he does, you won't interact with him."

"I promise. Are you mad at me?" She asks, softly.

"No. I'm just worried. I want you to do everything you can to stay safe."

She holds my eyes with hers. I wipe tears off her cheeks.

"I'm just tired of sitting and doing nothing. I feel like I'm sitting around and just waiting for something bad to happen. I want to do something." Her eyes light up as if letting out this bit of information brings her to life.

I can't help but smile at this spunk. I love the independent streak in her. "I understand that, but this isn't a game. I walk around with a gun on my hip and I have training to deal with the mentally ill, you don't. Please let me handle this."

I see the fire in her eyes, but she nods. I can tell she wants to argue. Her bright red hair falls in her face. My gaze is pulled down to the chain hanging around her neck and the golden charm teasing her bare breasts. When I pull my eyes back up, the fire in her brown eyes has dissipated and is replaced by tender emotion that draws my lips to hers.

"Thank you. When this is over, I'll take you somewhere nice, just me and you."

Her arms go around my neck and I inhale the sweet scent of her perfume as we lay down. She curls into my body and rests her head on my chest.

"The alarm people and painters are supposed to come tomorrow to my house. I took the day off."

"I remember. I have to work, but promise me you will be safe. I'm paying someone to sit there and watch your house until you are done."

Her head tilts up and I press my lips to her forehead. "I didn't know you did that."

"I mean business."

She yawns and, soon, I hear her deep rhythmic breathing telling me that she's fallen asleep in my arms.

I have to think up a way to get rid of this guy. I have a feeling he won't go easily. The last thing I want is for Emily to turn into someone who's afraid of her own shadow. I'll be damned if I won't do everything in my power to protect her.

EMILY

Why can't I move?

My arms and legs feel like lead.

I taste the fear in my mouth like bile.

Turning my head, I see the shadow of a person standing beside my bed.

God, where am I?

Emily, Emily can you hear me?

I wake up thrashing and sweating. My heart still pounds from a dream that seemed so real I can't help but doubt my senses as I glance around Isaiah's bedroom. He's sound asleep beside me. At least I didn't wake him up.

My head hurts. This is the first time this has happened here, with him. I thought that part was over. With a deep sigh, I creep out of bed. My fear starts to fade as I head for the bathroom looking for something to take for the pain in my head.

Must be the stress. They say that it comes out in strange ways, but I always imagined myself strong. I didn't think I'd be taken down easily, but I suppose we all have our breaking points.

Chilled by the trek to the bathroom, I crawl back into bed and snuggle into his warm body. If not for Isaiah, I can only imagine the condition that I'd be in.

The next morning, I got the lecture of a lifetime before I left the apartment. Isaiah doesn't think I'm taking things seriously enough. He might be right, but I'm also inclined to believe that he's overreacting because he's a cop.

Thank God he doesn't know I had another nightmare.

He's paying an off-duty officer a lot of money to sit at the end of my driveway and keep Noah away from me and turn away any potential gift deliveries. We argued, and I lost.

Now I'm standing on my front porch for the first time since Sunday, staring at a patrol car while ADT drills holes in my walls and painters wait for them to finish so they can get started.

It felt good to be home, until I walked in the front door and saw the empty spaces left by my missing furniture. Let's not even talk about the words scribbled all over my house. I spent an hour trying to get the paint off my headboard, only to end up in tears. I ask the painters to trash it for me.

I guess Isaiah is right. There must be something seriously wrong with Noah to do something like this and then seem surprised when I tell him that it scared me.

How in the hell did he even get in here? I checked all the locks and windows again but didn't find anything. Maybe he knows how to pick a lock.

With nothing better to do, I decide to check the house for anything else suspicious. Maybe I will notice something that an officer wouldn't think to look for. I spend over an hour looking over every nook and cranny that I can find.

I scour my laptop and open up my browser history. That's when I see the first thing that alarms me. Someone opened up my student loan account weeks ago, and it wasn't me. It's not due yet. When I open it up, my mouth drops open. It's paid. Someone logged into my account and paid it weeks ago. Tears spring to my eyes as I sit at my dining room table staring at the time stamp. He used my laptop to pay this off. The activity is clear in the browser history.

How long has he been coming and going in my house?

Has he been watching me?

Nausea rolls into my stomach as I look around, wondering where he might have been hiding. My sick stomach falls into my feet when it occurs to me that there is one place that I never thought to check. The attic.

Rising to my feet, I close my laptop and pocket my phone as I walk to the door in the hallway that leads up to the one part of the house that I've never used. After opening the door, I flip on the light that illuminates the attic from the bottom of the stairs. I swallow, staring up the staircase looming before me. *What if he's here now?* Maybe I should wait.

Being cautious, I return to the kitchen and retrieve a large kitchen knife, and then head back to the attic. This time, I take the stairs carefully, my eyes darting and my knife at the ready in my hand.

Once at the top, I do a full 360 before I allow myself to breathe again. He's not here. I wonder if he hid up here. Maybe he only came in when I wasn't home.

Unable to spot anything strange right away, I press onward. I'm careful to step on the beams of the unfinished floor. I should lay floors up here and turn it into a room, it would work as an extra bedroom or a game room or something. I file the idea away as I move from corner to corner, searching for anything off.

That's when I see it. There is a lump in the insulation in a dark corner. I shine the light from my phone to the area, but I can't tell what it is. Once I get there, I wish I'd never found it. I crouch, move the insulation, and find a small, digital camera.

Fuck.

Tears flood my eyes and bile rises in my throat as I pick it up and turn it on. It still has enough of a charge to spring to life. Oh God.

I stand on trembling legs, sweat dripping into my eyes thanks to the heat up here. I head back down the stairs and look around at all the people moving around in my house. The ADT guy approaches me and he shows me how to use the system. I sign his paper with a trembling hand.

I head outside to be alone before turning the camera back on. Sitting on my porch, on the porch swing that I hardly use, I work through the menu as I cry.

With a shaking finger, I hit play.

My hand flies to cover my mouth to stifle a sob as I watch myself, filmed from above.

Dressing.

Walking around the house.

Playing with Maxie.

Vomit rises in my throat; the acidic taste of bile floods my mouth.

Sleeping.

Showering.

In the throes of orgasm.

The one that makes me bend over the rail and heave my breakfast into the yard is the last one I can stand to watch. It's night time and I'm sound asleep. The camera is placed on my dresser and a dark figure, a man, whose face I can't see, is walking around me. The figure carefully pulls back the covers to reveal my naked body. He touches me, unzips his pants, and eventually comes into a pair of my panties.

I turn the camera off and set is aside, unable to look any longer. I can't even process what I've seen as terror sickens my empty stomach.

It isn't until now, when it's too late, that I realize I never should have touched this camera. I probably ruined all his fingerprints. God, Isaiah was right. This guy is dangerous. Suddenly I'm scared to death and looking over my shoulder. *Is he always watching me? Has he been in Isaiah's apartment too?*

No, that can't be. No one knows I'm there.

It's as if the fear that I wasn't feeling all this time suddenly catches up with me and I'm terror stricken.

The cop at the end of the driveway is talking to someone in a flower delivery truck. A fresh sob escapes me when I see the delivery guy standing there with a massive bouquet of flowers, which is turned away.

How did he know I would be here today? How much does he know? Has he been watching me for months?

I dial Isaiah. This is so much worse than I thought.

"Hey sweetie, how is it going?" His chipper voice only makes me cry harder.

"Isaiah, I found..."

"Hey! Hey what's wrong, are you okay?"

I shake my head no, as if he can see me. "I found a camera in the attic. Please, can you—"

"I'm on my way. Is he on it?"

"You can't see his face. There's no way to tell who it is. I can't believe, oh God, I'm going to throw up again."

I drop the phone and heave again over the side of the porch; sobs shaking me as I vomit.

I'll never be able to live comfortably in this house again. I'm going to have to sell my home.

"Emily," he's calling my name when I pick up the phone again.

"I'm here, sorry."

"Baby, what's on it? You don't sound like you are okay." His voice is heavy with worry.

"Just come and see for yourself. I can't even say it."

Isaiah comes pulling up in an unmarked, black Lincoln town car. There is a determined purpose in his steps as he crossed the yard to me. Reaching me, he takes the camera and pulls me into his arms.

"I'm here, it's okay. Come sit in the car with me."

Moments later, I'm sitting in the seat beside him as he watches the same videos that I just watched. His brow is furrowed and his face grows red as each sickening moment is exposed. I'm still crying, curled up into a ball against the door as if it can protect me from the horror that is on that camera.

"I can't believe this. I can't believe he left this behind. He must have been expecting you back. God I'm going to fucking murder him." He whispers the words as if talking to himself.

The whisper sends a chill through me, all the way down to the bone.

Looking up, Isaiah meets my eyes. His eyes are angry.

"What do I do now?" I choke.

"We are going to add this to your harassment report, for starters." He holds my eyes for a long moment, and then turns the camera off. "He's been watching you and filming you for weeks. Maybe longer." He casts his gaze out the window as he runs a hand over his blond head.

"I can't live here. I can't. I'll always think someone is watching me."

He grabs me by my arms and pulls me against his chest. His voice is a rough whisper into my hair. "You can live with me. I'll get an alarm installed. I'm so sorry, Emily. Fuck. I'm going to kill him for this."

I clutch at his shirt, burying my face in his scent for comfort. "You can't kill him. Please don't get into trouble. I need you." I've never needed anyone before.

"I can't sit and do nothing. There has to be a way to get to him, and to stop this. You are moving in with me, you hear me? You won't be coming back here. I'll get your stuff moved and stored for you."

I lift my head. I'm so close to his face that I feel his breath touch my lips.

"Move in? Like forever?"

"Yes."

"But—"

He silences me with his lips. A hungry, desperate kiss, as if he's claiming my lips for his. It settles the nausea in my gut and stills my pounding heart. When he pulls back, I look up into desperate, gorgeous copper colored eyes and nod.

It's crazy. Moving in with him this soon. Moving out and selling my house. It's insane. This whole situation is complete madness. But Isaiah loves me. It's all over his face with an unspoken plead. He's silently begging me with a look. I can't ever live here again. I can take the money and buy a new house. Maybe with Isaiah. "Okay then. I'm going to sell this place; I can't even look at it again after this."

I don't even know how I'm going to be able to go back to work now. I'm going to be terrified to cross the parking lot. Scared that every time I look up, he will be there.

Are things ever going to be normal again?

CHAPTER 14

EMILY

Later, at home, I change into something comfortable and sit heavily on the side of the bed. I'm painfully numb. There are too many thoughts bouncing off the walls of my skull.

Isaiah walks in, leans on the doorjamb, and crosses his muscular arms over his chest. "I called ADT, but they can't get here for a week and a half to do the install. I talked to the apartment manager. She said it's fine as long as I get it removed when I move out. I also ordered pizza while you were in the bathtub. It's here."

I look up into his eyes with heaviness in my chest. "Thanks."

He considers me for a moment, and then joins me on the bed. Taking my hand, he laces our fingers together. His hands are hot.

"Tell me what you're thinking."

His thumb caresses the back of my hand. "I don't know. Just thinking about everything. I don't want to sell my house. I don't want to be scared."

"It's okay to be scared, and no one said you have to sell your house."

I inhale and exhale.

"How can I walk around in that house after seeing what's on that camera?"

"The same way I'm sitting here instead of driving to Noah's house and shooting him on sight. We do what we must. You can rent the house until you are ready to move on."

I glance up at him. He has kind eyes and inviting lips. "You think so? Rent it out?"

"Yeah, why not? We can store your stuff. That way it's not permanent. I don't want you to make a big decision like that based on pure emotion. There is too much going on right now for you to make a choice like that. This way you have some time to breathe."

"I've been looking over my shoulder all afternoon. I feel like I'm being watched now. Do you think that will fade?"

Leaning in, he kisses my forehead and then touches his forehead to the place he kissed. "Someday it will. You know I love you."

His words still my heart and calm my breathing. I love him too, so much, so fast. I never knew that it could hit me this way. He's like a tidal wave that engulfed me and I'm floating on the currents of his sweet kisses.

"I love you, too."

After a moment, he speaks again. "I'm going to make it a point to be around when you get off work for a while. Sitting close by when you head home. Make sure you check your car before you get into it: under, front seat, back seat, and the trunk. It's okay to be overly cautious and a little paranoid in a situation like this."

"I will. Have you talked to anyone at work about all this?"

"Just the patrol officer that took the initial report. I showed him the tapes and he said he'd make sure it gets assigned to a detective ASAP. They will be calling you. I never did talk to my sergeant and ask her how she knows him. It's best that we let the evidence do the talking and not push them towards him. It makes us look bad when we do that. Unfortunately, he is smart and resourceful and isn't leaving behind much. I can't believe that he left that camera."

Standing up, he grabs both my hands and pulls me to my feet. "Come on, baby. Let's go have pizza and beer and watch some TV."

I smile at him. He grins back, tugging me along as I drag my feet.

NOAH

I pace my living room, the bamboo floor cold under my bare feet, and I chew on my nails. I can't believe I screwed up. The camera was gone. I went back for it today, and it was gone. Someone found it. I have copies of the footage; so, I know that I'm not recognizable, but damn it.

I wonder if it was Emily or that stupid cop who found it. And the flowers I sent to her today were sent back. The company told me that there was an officer in uniform that turned the delivery away. This means that she never got the check that I stashed in the card that came with the bouquet, which was intended to replace all her things and pay for the damage to her house.

I'll have to resort to something else. I walk down the hallway and open my bedroom door. The picture I have of Emily smiles at me from the frame beside my bed, as I walk past it. Opening a door, I walk inside and look at Emily's side of the closet. I've hung up all the clothes I bought her, stored lacey under things in drawers, and piled boxes and boxes of shoes.

Time to pack all this up. I can't wait anymore. Things are spiraling out of my control. It's time to either get the cop out of the way or push forward with my plan. The house I've prepared is ready. No more waiting.

I run my hand over dress after dress hanging in the closet, knowing that soon they will be as close to her skin as I will be. I pause on my favorite. A white silk backless dress, with thin straps and a plunging neckline. I set it aside. Opening a drawer, I choose white, lace panties to go with the dress, and then I pick out shoes and accessories.

My pulse rate picks up and my breathing quickens as I imagine her slipping into this dress. The way it would hug her hips and reveal just enough of her breasts for me to admire. She's going to look so sexy.

I place the dress on my bed. This is the one I want her to wear for me on our wedding day. I'll handle this dress myself. I message my assistant about the rest. She will take care of them for me.

We are going to be so happy together.

After I place my favorite in a white dress box, along with the panties and jewelry, I take the box and the shoes and put them back in the closet, away from the rest.

Glancing at my watch, I see it's close to eleven. I get into my black Corvette and pull out of my garage, careful to close the gate behind me. The drive from my house to Isaiah's isn't long, but finding a place to park my car out of sight proves more difficult. I need to be able to sit in it to watch for him to leave, but be out of sight at the same time. I've been here every night since I found out where he lives, waiting and hoping that he will get called away so that I can go in and see my Emily. I find a spot around the corner, pulling in backwards. Grateful for my heavily tinted windows, I watch the cop's car, hoping that he is called out to work tonight. It's a shame that the blinds are closed.

I miss her. She must miss me too. I wonder why she didn't call me today.

Picking up my phone, I dial her for the tenth time today. It still goes straight to voicemail. I leave a message, one of many I've left today. "Hi Emily, I'm getting worried about you. I haven't heard from you, or seen you, in a while. Please call me so I know that you are okay."

I know she's home with him. My gut churns. He's looking at her and touching her. He's kissing lips that are mine. Emily is using his shower and sharing his bed, but I know she's laughing at him. I grit my teeth as the light in the front window of his apartment goes out, and the bedroom light goes on. She can't want this, him. This isn't her.

There must be a reason she's here with him. Maybe she's afraid. Maybe she needs me to save her. My heart starts to pound as I realize that she might be there against her will. This explains everything. The reason she won't answer my calls, and the reason she moved out. Maybe he told her to tell me that I scared her. He already threatened me. Maybe it's not a test at all. *What if she needs me to rescue her?*

I look at my watch. It's already midnight. Too late for a call to Julie. I'll speak to her first thing in the morning.

Emily will be so grateful when we are finally together. I slip into one of my fantasies as I sit and watch the window until the light blinks out. I imagine Emily smiling at me, gushing over the white dress, and teasing me with sultry glances as I tell her how beautiful she looks. She would invite me to dance with her. After a while, I would slip the dress off her shoulders. I can hear her voice in my ear, asking me to take her.

I sit in the parking lot until I can't hold my eyes open for another moment before I finally give in and go home.

I slip into my bed. My eyes are on her picture as my lids close. Tomorrow, I'll talk to the police and give Emily the chance she needs to get away, so she can be with me.

I know she wants me. When she said my name on the phone, I felt it in her voice. She's too shy to tell me.

ISAIAH

Looking into her eyes is what keeps me sane. I really want to load my gun and drive over to that bastard's house and end this right this minute. I haven't ever felt anger like this before.

I'm damn near helpless. All I can do is try to keep this all within the confines of the law, and hope that it's enough to stop it, eventually. There are stalking laws on the books now, but they are damn near impossible to prove. And good luck getting the District Attorney to press charges even if you do think you have enough evidence to move forward.

Emily sits cross legged on the couch sipping on a cup of coffee when I tell her that I'm going to take a shower. She smiles at me and tells me that she will meet me in bed.

In the bathroom, I step into the steaming hot shower. Images of the video on that camera roll through my head for the millionth time today. I sure as hell didn't want to show it to that patrol officer, one of my co-workers. She's my girl. I don't want anyone to see her like this, ever. Now if this ends up in court, those tapes might be played in front of a courtroom full of people.

I didn't mention this to her. She wouldn't have let me submit the camera into evidence if I did. She doesn't need that little tidbit of information to stress her out now.

I rinse off and grab a towel, running it through my hair before I dry my skin.

All this bullshit is pulling my head away from where I really want to be. I waited for so long to find someone like her. She captured me with one look that day we met, and I can't even enjoy it the way I want to because of this lunatic.

I wrap the towel around my hips and walk out of the bathroom, flipping off the light. The living room is dark, but I check the lock on the front door. I look out the window for anything that doesn't belong. I check the front closets, hall closet, and every other place I can think of before I open my bedroom door.

Emily is sitting on my bed cross-legged, wearing one of my police t-shirts, frowning at her phone. It's the first time I've seen her help herself to one of my shirts and it stops me cold. I smile, frozen in the doorway for a long moment before I move again.

When I bounce down on the bed in front of her, she looks up at me with a smirk.

"I have to change my phone number. I blocked him, but he keeps leaving me messages."

She shows me the phone. I scan through about a dozen voicemail to text messages.

"I'll take this with me to work tomorrow. They can pull all these off the phone. I'll get you another one." I toss the phone aside. I'm tired of talking about him.

She must see it in my face, because she gives me a slow, knowing smile. "I know that look."

"I sure hope so. By now you should be pretty used to it." I grin, leaning close to her.

She giggles. It's a sound that I haven't heard all day. I didn't realize I was missing it until it touches my ears, sending my heart slamming against my ribcage.

"You look hot in this shirt." I pull her earlobe in between my teeth.

She laughs, leaning into me as I fall on top of her. "Then why are you pulling it off of me."

I laugh, pushing the shirt up, trailing kisses around the waistband of red panties. Emily wiggles, threading her fingers into my hair as I drag my lips up her belly, lingering at her breast exposed by the pushed up shirt. "You are so beautiful." I growl the words and I trace my tongue around the curve of a plump breast arched into my face as her breathing hitches.

The sounds she makes, the touch of her hand, the way she opens herself to me, and looks at me makes me dizzy. I could have her in my bed every moment of every day and never tire of her. Her red hair falls around my face when she shoves me onto my back, her legs wide around my hips.

I grab her face in both hands, pushing my hips up into hers until she groans my name. Her back arches when I slide my hands down her body and her head falls back in a beautiful moan. I can't take my eyes off her for a second. She has me mesmerized.

Eventually, we fall apart in the bed, breathing heavy and smiling. Our eyes meet and she grins at me. I crawl over to her, and she welcomes me with open arms as I nestle myself into her shoulder. Her pulse beats against me, slowing down until I hear her yawn.

"Isaiah, I love you."

I grin in the dark. "I love you back."

CHAPTER 15

NOAH

The next morning, I dress with precision. A new fire lit inside me at the thought of helping Emily escape the bounds of Detective Penrose. Surely, she's there against her will. This is the only reasonable explanation.

Standing in my closet, I smooth my black jacket before I button it over a crisp, black shirt and tie. My reflection smiles back at me and my black eyes alight with anticipation. Emily will be so grateful when she finds out that I did this for her. I open a bureau drawer and select one of a dozen watches. Carefully, I secure it to my wrist. It matches my cufflinks and tie clip. I want to look my best, in case I see her later today. Satisfied with my appearance, I grab my wallet and my phone, and head out.

The clerk at the desk smiles at me broadly when I approach her. Her eyes drift over my expensive suit and back up to my face with curiosity looming behind bright blue eyes. Once again, I have no trouble gaining access.

I find Sergeant Julie Barton just outside her office, smiling. Her shiny brown hair is down, just long enough to graze her shoulders. She grins at me and invites me in with a wave of her arm.

"Noah, what are you doing here today? I wasn't expecting you." She flops down in a worn, leather chair behind her cluttered desk.

I struggle to keep the smile on my face as the clutter everywhere makes me twitchy. I want to shove it all off her desk and onto the floor and explain to her that this is unacceptable. Instead, I relax my face and focus my gaze on her brown eyes.

"Are you ever expecting me? I like to keep you guessing." I tease.

She laughs. "True, that you do."

I drum my fingers on the arm of the chair. "I'm afraid this isn't a social visit. I need to speak to you about one of your detectives."

Her brow furrows as she leans forward with her elbows on the desk and her fingers clasped together. "Sounds serious. What's going on?"

"I have a friend; her name is Emily Bronte. I think she's in some trouble. I believe she's been seeing your detective, Isaiah Penrose, and I think he's abusing her."

Her face wrinkles and she cocks her head at me, pulling a legal pad out of the top drawer in her desk. She scratches down Emily's name. "That's a serious allegation, Noah. What has you thinking that? Has she said something to you? Did you see something?"

I glance behind me to make sure the door is shut. "She won't return my calls, and she refuses to accept my gifts. I think she's avoiding me because he's threatened her. She has lived alone for years and all of a sudden she moves out of her house and no one can reach her. Her friend Caroline works for me and she can't get hold of her either."

Julie scratches notes as I speak. She asks me for contact info on Emily and Caroline, which I provide. I see no hint of disbelief in her as she continues to ask me questions, and I answer them the best I can.

I need to do this, to help Emily.

"Is this the same woman you said was your girlfriend that day you locked your keys in your car?" She taps the pen on the notepad.

I smile. "Yes, that's her."

"You said she was your girlfriend that day."

I adjust my tie. "We have a complicated relationship. I know her, and I know that something is wrong. She wouldn't be doing this if it wasn't serious. Someone recently broke into her house and I offered to help her pay for the damage, but the money was turned away. Penrose had someone there guarding her; no one can get to her. Does that sound normal to you?"

She stares down at her notes. No hint of her thoughts on her face. Her eyes, as if made of stone, reflect nothing of what she's thinking about what I've told her. "I've seen that report, on her house. Someone has been stalking her; filming her for weeks. Did you know about that?" She doesn't look up at me when she speaks.

"I haven't been able to reach her to check on her. He seems to have her locked up pretty tight."

Of course, except for the days when I visit their apartment.

She nods. Looking up at me, she meets my gaze with a serious face. "These are some pretty serious things you are accusing him of. I am going to talk to Emily and get her side of the story and go from there. I have your info; so, if I need anything more from you, I'll be sure to call you."

Her tone tells me that the conversation is over. I smile. "Of course you do. You can stop by anytime you like."

A smile creeps onto her face as my flirtatious tone sinks into her ears. Julie and I have a history. It used to be one of those friends with benefits situations, until I met Emily. Julie got a long-term boyfriend and we stopped the sexual part of our relationship a while ago. It gave me an easy out without having to tell her about Emily.

"I'll remember that. Have you had lunch yet?" She stands up.

Lunch? My brow furrows. I have to bite my tongue not to ask her why she isn't shoving me out the door and running to Emily's workplace to ask her about the allegations. Emily needs the opportunity to tell the truth without that damn detective on her ass, scaring her into hiding from me.

Bad idea to tell her how to do her investigation.

"I wish I could, but I have to get going. Can I take a rain check?"

I linger after standing up. Julie walks around the desk and smiles into my eyes, her hand brushing mine. I bristle, trying not to let it show.

"Of course. Can I meet up with you after work, perhaps?" Seduction drips from her words.

I need Julie, so I have to play along. "You know where I am. What happened to your boyfriend?"

She rolls her eyes, leans into me, and touches my tie. Her hand rests on my chest. "I kicked him out. That's over. So..." she turns her eyes up to mine. "Is there still room for me in your bed?"

Emily will know that I did this to save her. She will understand that I had to do what I had to do, to get her away from him and back into my arms where she belongs. Julie knows that there isn't anything more to what she and I have always had. No harm, no foul.

I smile. She bites her lip as I tuck a lock of her hair behind her ear, my fingers lingering on her cheek. I let my thumb graze her bottom lip, and she sucks in a breath as her eyes darken with lust.

"What do you think?"

Whatever happens, I'll be thinking of my Emily the whole time.

I WAITED on pins and needles all day, with my eyes on my phone. Nothing. No call from Julie. No call from Emily. When I get home, I let a stream of expletives fly out of my mouth as I hang up on her voicemail without leaving a message.

After I change into a pair of gray sweatpants and a bright green Dri-Fit t-shirt, I walk into the kitchen and open an imported beer. I don't know how much more of this I can stand. I take a long, icy cold drink and set the bottle down on the black granite counter top just as my doorbell rings. I walk on bare feet to the front door, which I open without bothering with the peep hole.

"Evening." Julie smiles at me shyly.

She's wearing a little black dress, her hair is down, and she has on more makeup than usual. I can't say that I'm surprised to see her. I give her a smile. She walks past me, tucking her hair behind an ear as she walks inside. Her high heels click on my floor in rhythm until she stops and turns to me.

"Can I get you a drink?" I head to the kitchen.

"Please. Your place looks just like I remember it. You're such a clean freak." She laughs, following me into the immaculate kitchen.

I pull another beer out and pop the top before I hand it to her. Her eyes touch mine as she brings it to her lips.

"I know, my OCD gets a little crazy sometimes. It's easy since I live here alone to keep it clean."

She nods, watching me pick up my beer. I take another long drink. I suppose I should tell her how pretty she looks and how good she smells. The seductive things I know she wants to hear. If it were Emily standing here, it would be no problem.

I purposely drag my gaze up and down her body. Her breasts are shoved into a push up bra, giving her a splendid amount of cleavage, in a dress that almost seems to be too tight on top. Following my gaze, she arches her back just right, pushing her breasts further out. Her finger dances around the lip of her beer.

"I like that dress." I stare. She takes a deep breath and steps towards me.

"I hoped you would. Seems you've been working out." Reaching up, her fingers slip over my bicep.

I have, actually. When Emily sees me for the first time, I want to please her. Being so much older than her, I realize that the money and distinguished good looks only go so far if you're flabby when the clothes come off. I want Emily to look at me with this same wanton desperation that Julie does.

"I have. I put a gym in the back of the house."

Placing her beer on the counter, Julie moves closer to me, her fingers brushing my forearm and then moving to my chest. Her blazing brown eyes are locked on my face. I can't deny the attraction. Not to mention my sexual frustration from watching Emily, naked and in so many positions, for all these months. It would be nice to close my eyes and imagine her under me while I'm on top of a real woman.

She's never been one to waste time. Julie doesn't have any problem with expressing what she wants to me when we've come together in the past. It's been a while, but she hasn't changed.

If this were Emily... the words echo in my head as I stare down at this hungry woman. I would take her and have her against the wall. I would make her come against my body as I thrust her until she screams my name. I would have this dress ripped to shreds, and she would beg me to do it again.

I get rough. Julie knows this. It's why she has always come back. She told me that I'm the first man who has ever just taken what he wanted and made her thirsty to have it done again and again.

Gently, I touch her hair. As I trace the line of her jaw, her eyes drift closed and a sigh escapes her lips. My fingers dance down her neck and to the swell of her breast. I palm them, in turn. I slide my hand up her neck, into her hair, grabbing a fist full of it and giving a hard tug that widens her eyes.

She gasps, but her eyes give away her lust.

I lean close to her ear. "Is this what you want?" I whisper.

"Yes, sir."

I smile. She remembers our game.

"Tell me."

She pants the words. "Please, sir."

Shoving her back, the blood rushes through my body, making me grateful that I'm wearing comfortable pants as I grow engorged.

"Take off your dress."

She stumbles, just catching herself before she falls down. She moves to take off her shoes.

"Not the shoes."

Gripping the hem of her dress, she pulls it over her head. She stands before me in nothing but a hot pink, push up bra and high heels. I shoot her a wicked smile. Her joy at my pleasure reflects in her eyes, but she doesn't smile.

"Ah, she's a bad girl. No panties, officer?"

A grin tickles her lips, but doesn't land.

"No, sir."

I stare at her openly, enjoying the tightness of a body that's pushed to its limits on a daily basis in the gym. How I've missed this. I have forgotten the surge of adrenaline I get from a woman ready to cower at my feet and begging to please me with wide eyes.

I move, circling her, but not touching her. She whimpers when I reach up, freeing her breasts from the bra in one move.

I pull off my shirt, and then lean close.

"Do you want me to fuck you?"

"Please."

"Please what?"

"Please fuck me, sir."

I grin, pleased. "On your knees."

Instantly, she drops. I release myself from my pants, and she groans at the sight of me. I grab her by her hair, with a hard fist, and a sharp cry of pain escapes from her pretty lips.

"Take it."

And she does. As she works me, I look down on her with a moan. It's Emily here, on her knees begging for me, not Julie. It's a red head I see bobbing back and forth, not a brown one. It's Emily's tongue flicking over every inch of me, begging to taste more of me and moaning when I pull her hair. I see Emily on her knees; her hands with a tight grip on my ass pulling me farther into her mouth.

My knees almost buckle. With a jerk on her hair, I find my voice again and push the words out on a groan. "Get up."

As soon as she rises, wiping her mouth, I push her into the wall. Her shoes fall off when I pick her up, holding her hard against the wall, thrusting roughly into her. I groan, a cry of pure pleasure as I take her.

I hear Emily's groans and her voice begging me to go harder. I feel her nails dig into my back and her legs wrapped around my hips. I'm thrusting her so hard that it must hurt, but she just begs for more.

Sweat slicks both our bodies, but we just keep going. She comes around me, and I almost groan Emily's name when I feel her tighten on me, her body bowing as she screams, racked with rolling ecstasy.

Her grip on me sends me blindly into the depths of one of the biggest orgasms of my life. I have to grit my teeth to keep Emily's name from breaking out of my throat as I ride it to the edge.

Julie falls slack against me, her head on my shoulder. "God, Noah. I swear you're even better than before."

I kiss her forehead. "You too."

When I look down into her face, I feel like pushing her off me. I want to throw her clothes at her and tell her to get out.

Thanks, I enjoyed the ride.

Instead, I pull her into the kitchen and hand her a bottle of water. I know she's not going anywhere. She will want more.

It's okay. When I look at her, all I can see is Emily.

CHAPTER 16
EMILY

I open my eyes and find myself in a bare room. It's dim. The only light comes from the window. It smells like a hospital. I gasp when I see him. Noah is sitting on the edge of my bed. He's holding my hand and watching me with sad eyes.

"Baby, do you know where you are? Can you hear me?" His voice is sad, almost desperate.

I can't move, my eyes are heavy, and I can't find my voice to scream.

I bolt up in bed. My chest heaves in the dark room as I try to catch my breath. Brushing angry tears off my face, I look around the room trying to figure out where I am.

Oh, that's right. Home with Isaiah.

Nightmare.

Leaning forward, I rest my face in trembling hands as I will my brain to recover from the dream. No one is here. No one is watching me. I peek through my fingers. Isaiah sleeps soundly beside me on his stomach. Dim light shines through the blinds and lights up his face. His blond hair is disheveled. His lips parted in slow, deep breaths, a light snore is coming from his throat.

Leaning over, I find the t-shirt that Isaiah pulled off me hours ago and slip into it. The cotton is cool against my sweat-laden, damp skin. After flipping the pillow to the cool side, I lay back and rest my hand on his arm. Touching him brings me back to reality and out of the dream, which is now fading into a fuzzy memory.

Funny how even when the dream fades, the fear lingers still.

He shifts in his sleep, rolling onto his side. His eyes flutter open, unseeing, and close again as he curls his arm over my stomach. I move into him, absorbing his body heat as the sweat evaporates off my skin, chilling me.

I've tried to be strong. The woman that doesn't need anyone's help. Standing on my own two feet since I was eighteen years old. I put myself through school, graduated, and paid my bills. I've been proud to hold my head high knowing that I did it all on my own. I've always felt that I could handle anything that came my way.

I lay here, snuggled against this man. I laugh silently as his body heats mine. I've fallen for a damn cop—ever the hero, protective, selfless. A blue collar, beer drinking, pizza gobbling guy with a head full of blond hair and a smile to make girls sigh all over Texas. The opposite of who I thought I'd end up with.

Somehow, with him I don't feel the need to prove myself any longer. It seems to be acceptable that I lean on him, just a little bit.

ON THE DRIVE into work my new iPhone, courtesy of Isaiah, rings. Not recognizing the number, I hesitate, but my curiosity and the annoyance of a ringing phone gets the best of me. I swipe the screen just as I pull up to a red light in the early morning.

"Hello."

"Hi, Emily. This is Sergeant Julie Barton of the Katy Police. We met once, maybe you remember?"

"Yes, you work with Isaiah. I remember you."

"I need to ask you a few questions. Can I meet you sometime today? Maybe this morning?"

I flip my blinker, turning left. This must be about my house and the camera. It never occurred to me how many people might see it when I handed it over to Isaiah to turn into the police.

"Yeah, I'm sure I can get away for a bit. My boss knows what's going on; so, he should be alright with me taking a break."

"Good, I'll come by in about an hour then. You still work at the CVS on Main, correct?"

"Yes."

"Great. I'll see you soon then."

After hanging up, I toss the phone into the seat beside me with a sigh. On one hand, I'm happy to see someone taking this seriously besides Isaiah. On the other, the thought of speaking to a police officer about things going on in my personal life irks me. I'm used to being on my own, until recently that is. I've always dealt with my problems by myself.

This is the first time that I haven't been able to do that. Involving the police seems like too much, but I know it has to be this way. After seeing that tape, nothing's been the same. I close my eyes and I see the image of that shadow standing next to my bed watching me sleep.

My stalker has even found his way into my dreams now.

I pull into the parking lot of CVS and turn off my car. Isaiah told me to look around and pay attention to who is around me before I get out of the car. This is what I do. I glance around as I shove my keys into my purse and text him to let him know that I got to work safely.

I've always liked my job, but lately it's been less than enjoyable. All I do is stress about who's coming in the front door. I jump when my phone rings. I'm constantly looking behind me to see if anyone is following me. The other day someone walked up and put a hand on my shoulder, and I shouted and jumped so high that they laughed at me for the rest of the day.

My coworkers don't know what's going on. My boss knows a little, just enough. I don't want them to know that something like this is happening to me. I still find it hard to believe myself.

Just over an hour later, I see Sergeant Barton walk into the pharmacy. She's not in a uniform, but it's clear she's a cop. She's wearing khaki pants and a black polo with the police logo on the left corner. Her gun is hanging off her hip as she walks my way.

I glance around, making my excuse before anyone knows that she's here for me. I scoot out of the booth and intercept her in the shampoo aisle.

She smiles weakly at me. One of her brown hairs slips out of her ponytail and falls in her face. "Hi, can I call you Emily?" She shoves a hand at me, and I shake it.

"Of course."

Another half assed attempt at a smile. "Can we go across the street for a coffee?"

"Sure."

I follow her across the street to the coffee shop. She buys me a cup of decaf and we sit in a corner. She stirs her latte absently as she looks up at me.

"I had Noah Burrell in my office yesterday. Do you know him?"

I bristle, sitting up a little straighter. "Sort of. Seems he thinks he knows me." I mumble the last bit.

"And how about your relationship with Isaiah? How is that?"

The question confuses me. I sip my coffee, wondering what business my relationship with Isaiah is of hers.

"It's great. I don't understand what that has to do with my problem."

She nods, setting down the stirring stick. "Are you friends with Noah?"

"No. I'm not friends with him. I'm pretty sure he's the one stalking me."

Something strange flashes across her face as she looks down into her coffee. I cross my arms and sit back in the high back chair. The scroll work in the metal digs into my back.

She clears her throat and sips her coffee. "It seems he is under the impression that you two are close. He told me that he thinks you are in danger with Isaiah. How do you feel about that?"

If this woman wasn't a cop I'd be in her face for that. I take a deep breath as blood rushes in my ears. I remind myself that she's just doing her job.

"I think he's a fucking lunatic, that's what I think. He's been calling me and showing up at my job. He broke into my house and filmed me. Apparently, he made himself at home in my attic. Now he's accusing the most fantastic person I've ever known of hurting me? This is ludicrous. Isaiah is..." My voice breaks. I try to swallow the lump in my throat, but it rises and tears threaten my eyes. Sergeant Barton raises an eyebrow at me, and then her face calms into stone. "He's amazing. He treats me like a princess and he loves me for who I am. I love him. I don't even know Noah. We've talked here in the parking lot, that's it. I've never hung out with him, or given him any reason to think that we are anything other than passing acquaintances. Something is wrong with him."

Tears stream down my face. I don't bother to wipe them away. Falling heavily back in the chair, she clicks a fingernail on the table.

"I understand why you're upset. I have to ask these questions. I need to follow up on the accusations."

"Does Isaiah know about this?"

She meets my eyes with a sigh. "No, he doesn't. I wanted to talk to you first to see if there is any basis for it."

I lean forward. "Isaiah told me that you are friends with him?"

Her eyes give away the truth. She *is* friends with him. I don't get an answer. She sips her coffee, and then looks back up at me.

"He mentioned that your house has been broken into. Did either of you talk to him about your suspicions?"

I laugh. "Hell no. I've been doing everything I can to avoid him. The reason he knows is because he did it. Are you people ever going to be able to stop him? This is driving me crazy. I want my life back!" Of course, I leave out my phone call. No reason to point out my own naïve stupidity.

As I watch her, I wonder if she will actually be honest in her report about this, or if she will cover for Noah. The woman shifts here and there. She's uncomfortable. I have half a mind to throw a couple questions at her, but I leave it alone.

“So, what happens now?” I ask, finally.

“I’ll write this up. I have to go talk to Caroline. He mentioned her too. When that’s done, I’ll talk to Isaiah. I appreciate you meeting me today. Is there anything you would like to tell me, before we part ways?”

I stand up. “No.”

She nods and picks up her coffee. I toss the rest of mine in the trash. I don’t have the stomach for it anymore.

ISAIAH

When my cell phone rings and I see Emily's name flashing on the screen of my smart phone, a smile breaks out on my face. I glance up at my buddy, the patrol officer that's sitting across from me in my office and he rolls his eyes at me.

"Hey, baby," I answer.

The officer fakes a gag, laughing. I flip him off and he grins at me.

"Hi. Did you know that your Sergeant came to see me today?"

"Who, Barton? No, I didn't. She doing a follow up or something?"

She snorts out a sarcastic laugh. "You might say that. She asked me if you were abusing me, that's all."

"What?"

"Yep. Seems that our friend Noah told her that he and I are close friends and that he is worried that you are abusing me somehow. I told her the truth. I kind of chewed her out, honestly. I probably shouldn't have, but I lost it."

I rest my head on the back of my old leather chair, leaning back and staring up at the ceiling.

"Just what we need right now. Don't let it get to you. There isn't anything to it. His word doesn't mean a thing when there is no evidence."

"I don't trust her, Isaiah. She is his friend and she looked at me all funny when I asked her about that. I didn't see her taking notes or anything either. What if she is on his side? How do we really know what is going on between them?" Her voice is edgy.

"I've worked with her for years. I've never seen her do anything even remotely off when it comes to a case. Maybe she's looking into it off the record. If she opened up a case file then I might get sucked into an Internal Affairs investigation. She might be trying to avoid that."

Emily huffs on the line. I look over at my friend, Billy Watson. He's eyeing me with curiosity, making no move to walk out and eject himself from my private conversation.

"I hope you're right. Something just felt hinkey about the whole thing. I guess it's possible that I'm being paranoid, considering what's been going on. Maybe I read too much into it." She breathes out a heavy breath. "I need a night out."

I smile. "Funny you should mention that. My buddy Billy Watson is sitting right here and he was planning a little house party for Saturday night."

Billy jumps up and snatches the phone out of my hand before I can pull away from him. I watch him grin at me and take over the conversation with my girl. "Hi, this has to be Emily. I've heard so much about you... the man never shuts up about you... didn't he tell you that Saturday is his birthday? Well I hope you yell at him... don't get him anything he doesn't deserve it... my house, yeah just some friends... I can't wait to finally meet you girl..." He hands the phone back to me, sitting back down in the chair with a laugh.

"Hi, sorry..." I start.

"Isaiah, I can't believe you didn't tell me that it's your birthday. You are in so much trouble," she shouts in my ear.

I smile. This kind of trouble I don't mind at all. "I didn't think about it until stupid here walked in and told me that we were having my birthday party at his house."

"How old are you going to be?"

"Thirty-one."

She whistles in my ear. "Old fart."

I laugh. "Thanks, doll."

"It's fine. I still love you. Now I have to figure out what to get you."

"Don't worry yourself over it too much. Anything is fine. And hey, don't sweat anything Barton told you. I'm sure nothing will come from it."

Emily sighs loudly. "Well, I wish she was as interested in my stalker as she seemed to be in our relationship and how I know Noah. She didn't seem to care."

"She's not assigned to your case, anyway. Detective Patterson is on your case, and she's been looking into it. She won't contact you unless something develops. So, don't think that no one is doing anything. And by the way, I talked to the Captain about locking your file."

"What's that mean, locking my file?"

"It means no one can open the case report, or view any of the evidence, but the detective assigned to it and some supervisors. I don't want you to think that everyone can see that video of you."

"Oh. I didn't know that there was such a thing. I figured that anyone up there could look at it. I appreciate that. I didn't think about what I would feel like walking into a room full of cops on Saturday that have seen videos of me naked." Her voice is hushed.

"I can't even see it now. It's locked, honey. No one needs to be in your business but you."

"Thank you. I need to go, my lunch break is over."

"Okay. See you at home. Love you, girl."

"Love you back." There is a smile in her voice.

My chest is warm when I hang up and toss my phone on my desk. I don't imagine I'll ever get over hearing her say that to me.

Looking up, I stare into my friend's cocky face. "Why are you still sitting here? Don't you have a job to do?"

He laughs. "You're not the boss of me. I'm just eavesdropping on all your drama, that's all."

"I can't wait for all this shit to be over. She's so stressed out. Finding out that someone's been in her house watching her has made her a nervous wreck. She's so damn jumpy."

He nods, his face relaxing into a sober sort of compassion. "I can imagine. It sucks. I've never heard of a case like that around here in the recent past. Maybe in Houston, but that's the kind of crap you hear about on that Investigation Discovery channel. Maybe you two will have your own Dateline episode."

I shake my head. "No thanks. Not the kind of attention she would ever be interested in. I've looked into it a little, but I almost got myself into big trouble a few days ago so I had to back off. I trust Patterson to do her best with it. I'll only get myself fired."

Billy nods. "You have more of a level head than I would. If Mags had someone stalking her and I thought I knew who it was, I'd be all over that shit."

I meet his green gaze across my desk. "I went to his house and threatened him."

His eyebrows go up. "No kidding?"

I nod. "Yeah. I'm surprised he hasn't told Barton about it since they are buddies. Maybe he's saving it for a rainy day or something."

He scratches the stubble on his chin, stands up, and adjusts his duty belt. The leather squeaks.

"Possibly. I don't think any of us here would blame you for it. We would all do the same thing if it was our family."

"Thanks. Keep it quiet though, would you?"

"You got it. I better get back to work. I have to make a phone call to a woman that's going insane over her neighbor. They've been having a property line dispute and they both refuse to mow this one foot strip of grass." He rolls his eyes heading for the door. "People and their perceived problems never cease to amaze me."

I lean back. "Job security, man."

"No kidding."

He walks out, closing the door behind him. Emily's words play over in my head again in the silence of my office. She said Julie acted funny. *I wonder, what kind of relationship does she have with this nut? I don't think she would ever cover up something for someone, but how can I really know?* It's not like I know her well. She's gone out with a few of us several times, but you don't get to know people that way.

I tap my pen on the table. I'm itching to dig deeper. I want to talk to Noah and Caroline. I want to go ask Barton point blank what in the hell is going on. Instead, I wiggle my mouse and my sleeping computer blinks, a case file staring back at me. I'm hoping to distract myself. I click on the evidence button and select the photos. Homicide scene photos should be enough to distract me. Too bad it's not.

CHAPTER 17

NOAH

Caroline stands in my office with her hands on her hips. Her face looks whiter than usual. The bags under her eyes aren't hidden very well by makeup and she looks thinner.

"You look like hell." I point out.

"Tell me about it. Gary is starting to wonder what is wrong with me. I'm a freaking mess. I have cops crawling all over me, Noah. What the hell have you dragged me into?"

"Lower your damn voice. What cops?"

"Well, Isaiah for one, but I already told you about him. Then some Sergeant called me today and left me a voicemail. I managed to avoid her call, but it's only a matter of time before she shows up asking me questions about something I don't even know about. I want to know what's going on here. What in the hell are you doing? You said you had this under control." Her voice cracks as she leans forward on my desk.

I lean back in my rich leather chair and smirk at her. "You do realize that you deal with cops for a living. Our whole business is about law enforcement. Don't you think you are being paranoid?"

Caroline sits down carefully in a buttery, brown leather chair across from me. Slowly, her legs cross.

"Of course, I'm not an idiot. I do know the difference between contacts and networking for business, and an officer that wants to question me. She mentioned you. I can't avoid her forever, Noah. And Penrose came right out and accused you of stalking her. You aren't being careful."

"So, what are you here for? To lecture me?"

"You swore to me that this wouldn't happen, that you... just fix it." She glares at me. "This isn't what Mom meant when she told us to take care of each other when he died."

I laugh, and she rolls her eyes at me. "You think that is what this is? Come now, baby sister. Our dead mommy has nothing to do with this. Take a deep breath and calm the fuck down. This is nothing."

Tears fill her plain brown eyes. "I can't be expected to lie to the police forever. This isn't right. You're dragging me into something I didn't sign up for. You said you wanted my help to meet her, to get with her, and I did that. Now this?"

With an eye roll, I lean forward. Clasping my hands on top of my desk, I let out a breath.

"Here is what you will do. You are going to tell that cop that Emily and I are friends. You will tell her that since she has been with Isaiah you haven't seen her, she's stopped calling you, and she won't accept your calls and that you are worried about her. Think you can manage that?"

"Emily said she doesn't know you. Are you going to hurt her?" Her voice is small. "And why would I do all this for you?"

"Why? Because you are my sister. Because you owe me."

She shifts, eyes down. She knows it's true. I saved her ass, something she can never repay.

"And no, I'm not going to hurt Emily. I plan to give Emily more than she ever dreamed of. I'm worried about how Isaiah is treating her. She hasn't been the same since she met him. I know Sergeant Barton very well. She won't hassle you. Next time she calls you, be available."

I get a slow nod. She pulls a tissue out of her designer purse and dabs her eyes. "How long are you going to hold this over my head?" She asks softly. Looking up, she meets my eyes.

"Caroline, do you trust me?"

"Of course."

"Then shut up."

"You have to promise to protect me, if something goes wrong. The police..." she says, quietly.

"Of course. Don't worry about the police. I'm not doing anything wrong. I won't put you in danger."

Our eyes meet again, and she stands up. "Fine, but if I get into trouble, I'm not going alone."

I laugh at her. "Get out of my office. I'll call you when I need you."

She sniffles and walks out, closing the door softly behind her.

TWO DAYS LATER, I'm leaving my office to go to Emily and Isaiah's apartment. It's Friday afternoon and they shouldn't be home yet. The apartment has me irked. I haven't been able to maintain the contact I had with her before. I drive gripping the wheel until my knuckles are white. I parked my black Corvette in the garage, fearing that someone might recognize the car. It's not easy to hide in an apartment building parking lot, especially in a flashy sports car. I pull into the parking lot in a new, slate gray Toyota. It blends in nicely, but doesn't have the pickup that my other car does.

Glancing down at my ringing phone, I see Julie's name. Maybe she has news for me. "Hi." I look up. Isaiah's blinds are closed again. Damn it.

"Hi there." Her voice is low and sultry. "Are you at home?"

"No, I'm running an errand. What do you need?"

"Oh... I was hoping to talk."

"We can talk now. Is it about the investigation?"

"I'm still working on it. I talked to Emily. I tried to get Caroline on the phone the other day, but I couldn't reach her. I haven't been able to try again. I've been swamped."

"What did Emily say?"

She coughs. "I'd rather wait until I have all the information, Noah."

"Julie, if this is about sex..."

She sighs. "I can't deny that I've been thinking about it since we met up. You're terribly addictive."

I shift in my seat. I can't deny that I feel the same way. Sex with Julie is powerful. She can take everything that I give her and begs for more. I look up at the apartment again.

"I can meet you this evening, at my place."

"Okay. Can I bring anything?"

"No, just don't be late. I don't like to wait. Eight o'clock."

"I'll be there." Her answer is breathy.

"I know you will." I hang up.

Glancing around, I get out of the car. Quickly, I rush across the parking lot on swift feet. Reaching the door, I find that the key still works. A breath of relief rushes out of my lungs. Any day now they might realize that it wasn't Isaiah that locked his keys in his car and I might be locked out again.

The apartment isn't as neat as it was a couple of weeks ago. Seems that Emily is rubbing off on him. I grit my teeth, looking around at his and her clothes on the floor by the couch. Maxie runs around my feet, wiggling happily. I ignore her.

This detective is in my way. I'd plant a camera in here, but I'm too worried that he would spot it. Moving through the house, I head into the bedroom. Laying down on her pillow, covering myself with her blanket, I close my eyes and I breathe in her scent. She will be in my arms soon.

JULIE IS RIGHT ON TIME. I open the door and find her with an eager smile, wearing black slacks and a lacey burgundy top. Her hair is pulled back into a loose ponytail. Leaving her shoes at the door, she enters in stocking feet.

Staring up at me with hopeful eyes, she smiles again. "Hi there."

"Come sit down."

I lead her through the front foyer to the white sitting room. I have a bottle of wine set out. Julie helps herself.

"Tell me what Emily said."

A shadow passes over her face. "Do we have to talk about this right now?"

"Yes, we do."

After throwing back her wine, she reaches for a refill. "She said you aren't friends. She said she doesn't really know you, and she's happy with Isaiah."

I stretch my arms across the back of the loveseat, watching her fidget on the wing chair.

"That doesn't surprise me at all. I didn't think she would admit to anything. I'm sure your investigation will uncover the truth."

"I'm sure it will." She holds my eyes.

Julie is a smart woman. I know what I'm risking. I also know how addicted she really is to me. I have a hard time believing that she will do anything other than do what it takes to stay on my good side.

She should be grateful that she's never experienced my bad side.

"You will let me know when you speak with Caroline." I stand up, motioning for her to follow me.

"I can. I haven't talked to Isaiah yet either."

We pass from the sitting area into the hall. I turn to Julie abruptly in the hallway, startling her. "Tell me honestly. Are you with me on this?" I step closer to her.

Mesmerized by me, she blinks slowly, her lips parted in a breath. Then she finally answers me. "You mean this Emily thing?"

"Yes, that's what I mean."

"Can I ask you why you are so hung up on her?"

"Does it matter?"

"I guess not. I don't care much about Emily and Isaiah. We aren't close. I don't know the woman. Can I ask you a question now?" She reaches out and touches my chest. "Will you kiss me?"

I chuckle. I've never kissed her, ever. She's asked me this before, half a dozen times. "No, we fuck. That's it. I'm not going to kiss you."

An instant pout curls her lips down. "But Noah—"

Leaning down, I grasp her top in both my hands and rip it open. She gasps as I push her against the wall and cup her chin in one firm hand. "This isn't enough for you? I don't have more to give you, Julie."

"Do you love someone else?" Her eyes search mine, as she starts to work the buttons on my shirt.

"Yes, I do. It's never bothered you in the past, who I loved and who I didn't. Does it bother you now?" As if I cared if it did.

She pushes my shirt open. Her hands move to my belt. "No, I don't care. I just want..." She trails off, opening my pants.

I grin at her. Her blouse hangs off her shoulders in tatters. I look down as she relieves me of my pants, holding me in her hand. Blood rushes and throbs in my veins thanks to her skilled touch.

"You just want what?"

She lifts her brown eyes from my crotch. "I want in your bed."

"Then you won't ever ask me again. You won't ever question me. Got it?"

Her eyes dim and darken with lust. She's beyond addicted. I have no doubt that she's never going to betray me.

"Yes, sir."

"That's my girl."

I allow her to look into my eyes for a moment. Then I grip her by her forearms and spin her around. Forcing her pants down her legs, I thrust her thighs apart with my thigh. As I push inside her, she cries out, her face pressed into the wall.

When I look up from her tight round ass, I see a shock of red hair. My Emily. I stroke her slowly and nuzzle her neck. She purrs, my Emily. I knew she would. "Emily, baby." I groan into her shoulder, nipping her with gentle teeth.

"Noah—" Julie's voice startles me. It pisses me off. I pull her hair and stroke her harder. Damn her for taking my Emily away.

"Noah you're hurting me—"

I grip her hips, roaring. I want Emily back.

She claims I hurt her, but she comes anyway. She convulses against the wall, and I follow right behind her. When she turns over her shoulder at me, I see tears on her face.

"Don't cry. You said you were okay with this." I feign sympathy, wiping her tears away in a rare show of gentility.

Julie looks down, as if embarrassed. "Just don't call out someone else's name and we can keep pretending."

"Pretending?"

When she looks back up at me, there is a hint of anger in her eyes. "Yes, pretending that you care how I feel. Pretending that I don't know all I am is a piece of ass. Pretending."

I shrug, bending to pull my pants up. "Whatever you say, doll."

CHAPTER 18
EMILY

Isaiah buckles the birthday watch on his wrist with a smile. "I love this. It's fantastic." He glances up at me.

I shrug. "You like it?"

It has a large black face with no numbers, and a black metal band. I had the words *Love, Emily* engraved on the back.

"It's perfect. Thank you." Leaning in, he gives me a soft kiss.

"So, where are we going again?" Standing up, I turn and face the mirror. I am wearing jeans and a slim-fit, blue, cowl neck, light knit sweater with the sleeves pushed up to the elbows. Bending, I grab my brown leather boots from the floor.

"My friend Billy Watson's house. You will like them. His wife is great. Your ass looks amazing in those jeans, by the way."

I turn, checking my butt in the mirror. "You think so? I've been slipping on the squats. Someone is always tearing my clothes off me." He stands grinning behind me. I meet his eyes in the mirror.

Isaiah looks casual, yet still yummy in a red Henley shirt and black jeans. He runs a hand through his hair, smoothing his blond locks back off his face. His twinkling eyes and big smile cause my stomach to curl inside me.

"I can't help it. You're just irresistible." He moves in behind me and puts his hands on my hips. "Mmm, you smell good."

"Thank you. I'm really pretty excited about going. It's been so long since I felt free to relax and have a good time without looking over my shoulder. I know this is your birthday, but I think I really needed this."

"It makes my whole day to hear you say that. I want you to be happy and relaxed. This has to end someday and, when it does, we can celebrate any way you want."

I nod, turning around. "Let's get this party started, birthday boy."

HIS FRIEND BILLY lives in on a quiet, country road outside of the city limits. When we pull in, I see that there are a few other cars here, which makes me wonder how many people I'm going to be meeting. I also wonder how many of them will be cops.

The house is a really pretty, two story, Victorian-style farm house. It's painted in antique white with a porch that goes all the way around the house. When we get out of the car, we are greeted by a pair of yellow labs bounding across the yard. Excited to see us, they stop just short of us and wiggle at our feet. Isaiah scratches them both on the head, behind the ears.

"Hi, ladies." He pushes past them, looking over at me. "That's Daisy and Trixie. They are well-trained. Normally they are in the house, but I guess he kicked them out for company."

I glance back. They follow us up to the porch and lay down on two big dog beds at one end positioned beside a porch swing.

"They won't run away?"

"Nope. Years ago he trained them with one of those invisible fences. After getting a little shock once or twice, they never tried again."

He opens the screen door. It squeaks on its hinges. He knocks on the door. I'm a little nervous. I've never met any of his friends. Being so preoccupied lately, I didn't think about it. The way things are going, family will be next.

The door flies open. We are greeted by a tall, husky guy with military short, dark brown hair. He grins, a beer in one hand. His eyes move from Isaiah to me, and he lights up. "Finally, we get to meet her! You must be Emily. God, it's nice to put a face to the name. He never shuts up about you."

Isaiah laughs. "This is Billy, by the way."

Billy sticks his hand out. I assume he wants to shake my hand, but, instead, he grabs me and pulls me into the house. The inside of the house doesn't match the outside, funny enough. It's been totally renovated. The floors are wood. It doesn't echo when you walk like it normally does in an old house with a wooden floor either. The front door opens right into the living area. The walls are taupe colored, and there is a fireplace covered with river stones burning in the far corner. The furniture all matches. There are off-white, leather couch and love seat with navy blue accent pillows, and matching lamps at either end of the couch on two cherry wood end tables. The tables match a large, square coffee table, which matches a big entertainment center with a curved TV set in the center.

The air smells like vanilla. I see the candle burning on the coffee table is the reason for the lovely aroma.

"This is her, everybody. Emily. The one that stole our Isaiah's little heart." He presents me to about half a dozen people.

Two women pop into the room through a doorway. One is wiping her hands on a dish cloth with a grin. "Billy, what are you doing? At least let the woman get a drink before you embarrass her."

Isaiah steps up beside me, laughing. He shoves Billy away from me and puts an arm around me. "You met Billy. He's nuts. That lady is his wife. Her name is Magnolia; we call her Mags. That other woman is Karen. She's here with Miles; that one in the chair. These guys are Luke, Brian, David, and Elvis." He points them out one by one. They each grin at me, waving in turn. A couple of them tip their baseball caps. I can't help but laugh.

Mags rushes over to us with a smile. She's a petite Hispanic woman with long, black hair that hangs almost to her waist. "Girl, we are really glad to meet you. What do you want to drink? I'm going to bring out the food soon."

I smile, glancing at Isaiah. "Um, it's his birthday so I figured I would be driving tonight."

She shakes her head and steals me from Isaiah with a gentle tug. "Oh, no. We already made up the guest room for you two. You are staying the night; so, you can drink all you want. You both need a night to cut loose and have some fun with nothing to worry about. No is not an option." She pulls me into a warm hug.

I can't help but hug her back. What nice people. "Oh, really? That's so generous of you."

She releases me. "It's nothing. Isaiah is like family to us. These two have been friends since the police academy. If Isaiah loves you then you must be amazing."

Warmth seeps from my chest into my limbs as her kind words wrap around me. I should have known that Isaiah's friends would be this way. I come from such a different sort of people. I never expected to receive a reception like this. I suppose over time, as I wrap my life more and more around his, that will change.

"I'm not all that amazing." I snort out. I see Isaiah watching me with love in his eyes. "Don't let her lie to you, Mags." He grins.

"And you, happy birthday." She leaves me to go hug Isaiah. "I should be mad at you for not bringing her over sooner." She swats his arm.

"I know, I'm sorry. Tonight should make up for all that. Emily, what do you want to drink?" He walks on long strides towards a doorway that I assume leads to a kitchen.

"Surprise me." I shrug.

A few minutes later, he pushes a small glass into my hand. The liquid is almost black. I take a sniff, licorice. "What is this?"

Isaiah grins, tapping my glass with his. "Jager Bomb. Jägermeister and Red Bull." I look up into a face beaming with utter happiness. He's home here with these people and seems to be beyond thrilled to have his two worlds collide on his birthday.

"Do you like licorice?" I cock my head.

"I hate it. But I like these things, for some reason. Now, you have to toast me. It's my birthday."

We are suddenly surrounded by all the boys, some with beers, some with what looks like whiskey. "Toast!" I think it's Elvis that says it. His Texas drawl is heavy, and it makes me grin. "Toast him, girl."

I laugh, glancing around the circle, suddenly feeling like a woman surrounded by half a dozen of her big brothers. I hold up my glass and look up into happy, copper colored eyes. A smile lights up his whole face. "To Isaiah. I have to say, I can't believe I fell for a cop. Not even a regular cop, a damn detective. But here I am. And how many of you boys are cops?" Every hand goes up. I laugh out loud, and then continue my toast. "Well, I will say this: Isaiah, I am honored to be here with you on your birthday. Not only are you amazing, and sexy, smart and fun, but you are older than I am. Bottoms up."

They all laugh. Glasses clink and I down my drink. The boys hoot and catcall. Isaiah leans in and kisses me. "Thanks, baby."

"Anytime. And I love licorice." I grin, take his glass, and head into the kitchen.

The kitchen is lovely too. Glass front, white cabinets and a butcher block countertop line the room. In the center is a round table, which looks like pine. It's covered with iced down beers, and a few bottles: Jack Daniels, Jägermeister, and Malibu Rum.

"Can I help?" I set the glasses down in the sink. Mags turns to me. She's layering beef and chicken onto a serving platter. "Thanks, sure. I can always use help feeding these animals." She laughs. "See all that stuff there?"

I glance over to where Karen is standing. She is pulling paper plates and plastic silverware out of a bag. On the counter is a stack of tortillas, a tray of sautéed onions and peppers, and a big bowl of Spanish rice. On the opposite corner is a big birthday cake. The sight of it makes me grin. "Yes."

"Just grab whatever and haul it out there. You can set it on the coffee table. I think the boys are setting up the karaoke machine."

My eyebrows go up. "Karaoke?"

She laughs. "Yes ma'am. It's a blast. No one can sing, don't worry."

I move, picking up the bowl of rice and the stack of tortillas. "Oh goodness. It's going to take a bit of booze to get me to sing."

She smiles warmly at me, putting the now empty cooking pan into the sink. "No worries there. I have faith in you." A wink is shot my way.

Two of the guys rush to Karen and me to relieve our food-laden hands. Isaiah and Billy appear to be setting up the machine. Isaiah is stringing two microphones across the room as Billy fidgets with the controls on the TV.

This is going to be a fun night.

An hour later, we've eaten our fill and helped clean up. Isaiah sits hiding his face like a seven-year-old boy as we all sing happy birthday to him. The cake is a raging inferno under thirty-one candles. I can't stop laughing and taking pictures of him as he hides his face, and then blows out the candles.

Moving to his side, I lean in. "What did you wish for?" I ask.

He grins, not looking at me as he pulls the candles out of the cake and tosses them onto an empty paper plate. "I'll show you later. I brought my handcuffs in case it comes true."

I blush, wondering who heard him, and then I laugh. Handcuffs. *Is he joking?* I can't believe it never occurred to me that he owns a pair of handcuffs. That just might be fun.

Glancing up at me, he meets my eyes and gives me a slow wink.

"I'm ready to sing… I'm first," I hear a male voice say.

A piece of cake is shoved at me, followed by a drink that smells like Malibu rum and pineapple juice. I accept them both, sit down on the couch, and tuck my feet under me. I kicked my shoes off fifteen minutes ago.

I feel at home with these people.

They sing, and sing, and sing. It's the funniest thing ever. Isaiah sits on the couch beside me. He's pressed right up against me until Billy gets up and tosses him the microphone.

"It's time." Billy smiles, scrolling through the songs.

Isaiah leans over and kisses me. "I hope you don't love me less after what you're about to witness."

I laugh. "Never. Could never love you any less."

"Ah, she's got jokes, ladies and gentleman." He says into the microphone, his voice booming in the house.

Billy settles on the song, and I bust out laughing just as Mags and Karen come sit with me. "Girl, watch these two. It's the funniest thing ever." Mags laughs.

"Yeah," by Usher.

You've got to be kidding me. When the music starts up, the grin that splits my face open is amazing. Isaiah turns and grins at me, bouncing his head up and down.

Billy sings the Usher part, and Isaiah sings the background stuff. It's the funniest thing I've ever seen. Towards the end, Billy bends over and starts twerking. Then Isaiah moves in and spanks his ass and the two dance in a grind that has the whole room rolling with laughter. I have tears in my eyes I'm laughing so hard.

"Girls turn!" Karen jumps up. Billy and Isaiah toss the microphones our way.

I shake my head, but I'm pulled to my feet by them both. Karen shoves one of the mikes into my hands and I roll my eyes. Mags is scrolling for a song.

Scanning the room, I see Isaiah sit down in the recliner. Our eyes meet across the room, and my heart explodes. He smiles a slow, lazy smile at me. He mouths I love you. I touch my chest where my heart is. My God, do I love him too. This is like that forever kind of love. I can feel it. I see it in his eyes as he stares at me across the room, stealing my breath. He loves me.

It isn't until the music starts that I realize she picked our song: "Girls," by Beyoncé. I laugh. Mags sings the lead. Karen and I jump in. By the end of it, I'm bumping hips with Mags, my arm is locked around Karen's shoulder, and I'm singing for all I'm worth.

Best night ever.

Hours, and I mean hours, later, the party ends. I'm buzzed, and Isaiah has that glassy look. I follow Isaiah to the guest room. It's a nice room with a queen size bed made up with a plain green comforter. There is a hutch with a TV in it.

I hear a click. When I turn my head, I see Isaiah locking the door. He gives me a wild look, and I shake my finger at him. "What are you doing, we are guests in this house."

He shrugs. Reaching into his pocket, he pulls out a pair of handcuffs, letting them dangle on one finger. "Told you I brought them."

My mouth drops open. I back into the wall, shaking my head as I giggle. He struts towards me, cocky and licking his lips.

"Please tell me you have the key."

He reaches into his pocket and pulls out the key. "Right here, babe." He sets it on top of the hutch, where I can't ever hope to reach it.

"You can't be serious." I back away from him.

"I'm very serious." Reaching out, he catches me by the arm. Cold metal is slapped onto my wrist, clicking closed. He grins at me, shoving me towards the bed. "You have the right to remain silent, but I know you're a screamer, so I might have to gag you."

He pushes me down and sits on me, looping the cuffs through the rail on the headboard. "Anything you say can and will be used against you in a court of law. You have the right to an attorney." He drags my free hand up, securing it in the other side of the cuffs.

I'm now laying here, under him, my arms secured over my head. He looks down at me and starts to slowly unbutton his shirt. "If you cannot afford an attorney, one will be appointed to you."

My heart is pounding and I can't wipe the stupid smile off my face. He keeps going. He shakes his shirt off, then leans up on his knees to undo his belt. "At any time you may choose to exercise these right. Do you understand these rights that have just been read to you?"

He climbs off me. He pulls his jeans off, and in just his underwear, he moves to unbutton my jeans. His fingers graze the flesh on my stomach, shooting lightening through my body. He pulls my jeans down over my hips, taking my panties with them.

"Well, do you? Understand?" He asks again as he pulls my pants off at the ankles. I grip the rails in my hands as he leers at me.

"I do. Officer, can I ask you something?"

He looks at me with no smile. "Yes, of course."

"Are you going to strip search me?"

Lust darkens his eyes as he pulls my top up and relieves me of my bra. The sweater is pulled over my head and looped behind it to keep it out of the way. "I think I have too. Bad girls like you might be hiding something." He shoves off his underwear and climbs onto me, straddling me. "I'll have to be very thorough."

My heart starts to palpitate. My mouth waters. He slides his hands up and down my arms, over my neck, and through my hair. He meets my eyes as he palms my breasts, rubbing them. He moves off of me and slides his hands over my stomach and down my thighs.

He looks up at me and speaks using his cop voice. "Spread your legs."

I whimper, and he smiles. I part my thighs, and he breaths heavily.

"Are you going to do a cavity search?" I ask breathlessly.

He slides a hand up my thigh. "Damn right I am."

Higher and higher it goes. I'm gasping when he hits his target, caressing me with his skilled touch. He leans over and teases my lips with a feather light kiss as he works. I groan.

"Officer…"

"Yes ma'am."

"If I fuck you, will you let me go?"

He grins at me. I arch, brought off the bed by a sudden thrust of his fingers. In a flash, he mounts me. Suddenly, he's inside me and I'm dying to touch him. I wrap my legs around his hips, pulling him deeper. "Isaiah…" I gasp.

He finally kisses me, deep and soft. It's a slow, sexy kiss that pushes me to the brink of climax. I groan into his mouth. He has one hand cupping my ass and the other holds him up.

"Don't stop." I whimper.

"I couldn't if a train hit me... Shit..." He buries his face in my shoulder.

I explode around him, biting his shoulder to keep from screaming. I white knuckle the bed rails, careful not to strain against the cuffs. He keeps going, stroking me and loving me. He lifts his head to look down at me with tenderness that steals my breath.

"God, I love you so damn much." He groans, thrusting his hips in rhythm. His eyes overflow with emotion. They roll back with the pleasure I give him, rocking with him. Then he jerks, stifling a shout and bursts into me. I hold him tightly with my thighs, loving the way it feels when he comes on top of me.

He looks down into my face with a smile. "I guess I have to unlock you now."

"I love you, Isaiah. Seriously, a lot. And that was fun."

He laughs, rolling off of me. He retrieves the key and releases me. Immediately I reach out and touch him, dying to feel his skin under my hands.

"That was amazing. I know I've had a lot to drink, but I... When I'm with you, I feel like I'm whole. I feel like I found the woman that I've always been searching for in you. I'm home when I'm with you. I fell for you the first night. You bewitched me. You're amazing. I can't get enough of you. Beautiful and strong and... you're everything. I can't imagine my life without you now. I can't figure out how to say the things that you make me feel. Like I want to be around you all the time. I love the way you smell and the way you look when you sleep. I close my eyes and you find me in my dreams. Then I wake up and you are asleep in my bed, in my house. I would do anything for you. I'd move. I'd sell everything. I'd quit my job. I'd die to protect you. I just..." His voice fades out as he falls back on the pillow. "I love you, Emily."

No one has ever articulated anything like this to me before. My heart has burst into a million tiny pieces, and then come back together with his name on it. "Isaiah, that... you... I..."

He wipes tears off my cheeks, and then smiles at me. "Don't cry."

"I can't help it. What you just said... it was beautiful. I love you too. I feel the same way about you."

Popping up, he kisses me swiftly. I get up and turn off the light and we are bathed in darkness. He curls up behind me, kissing my shoulders gently as he pulls my body tightly to his.

"Happy birthday," I whisper.

"Thanks. Best birthday ever."

CHAPTER 19

NOAH

The sound of the shower running in my private bathroom is loud to my ears. I never let anyone use my bathroom. Now I'll have to get my maid to sanitize the damn thing.

Julie asked me nicely if she could take a shower; so, I let her. I walk naked into the bathroom. The steam from the shower sticks to my skin as I enter the room.

She's humming a tune that I don't know. The second thing I notice is the steam. My oversized bathroom is full of humid air and the steam rises in the open stall of the huge stone shower. Julie has her back to me, enjoying the spray of four carefully placed shower-heads. I was going to wait, but the more I think about it, the more I realize that the running shower will be helpful to me.

I flex my hands. The latex gloves cling to my skin, dampened by my own sweat in this spa like environment. My grip flexes around the knife handle. Keeping my eyes on her, I watch for her to turn.

Deep breath now. This is for Emily. It's the only way. Julie still hasn't talked to Caroline, claiming that she's been overwhelmed and unable to get back to it. I don't believe her. She's stalling for some reason.

It doesn't matter any longer. I'm done waiting. I step into the shower. The hot water hits me as I wrap one of my hands around her waist. My other hand has the blade. She giggles, leaning into me, until she realizes that I'm wearing gloves.

"Noah, what are you—"

I silence her by pushing the knife through the flesh of her throat. She gurgles and gasps and clutches at her throat as blood sprays the inside of my shower. The bloody mess mingles with the running water and the gore is rinsed down the drain. Julie turns and falls against the wall with wide, terrified eyes.

She can't ask me why. I crouch down and touch her face. I brush the hair from her eyes as she struggles to breathe.

"It's going to be okay." I lean in and kiss her lips as she tries to suck air into her lungs. "There is your kiss, sweetheart."

I watch the light fade from her eyes as the shower continues to wash her life off of my body and out of my shower.

I've never killed anyone before. I've also never had trouble getting to someone I love like I have with Emily. I won't be separated from her any longer. My patience for this situation is gone.

ISAIAH

I knew that I would regret letting Patterson talk me into swapping our on-call duty this week. It's three a.m. on Tuesday morning when my cell phone wakes me up. As I grab for it, I hear Emily mutter something I can't understand. "Sorry, it's work calling," I tell her as I answer the phone.

"This is Penrose." I struggle to sound alert.

"Detective, I'm sorry to wake you. There's been a death." The normally happy dispatcher is struggling to remain composed, alerting me to something bad.

"It's fine. What do you have?"

She rattles off an address, and then says, "Um, I hate to be the one to tell you this, but it's Sergeant Barton. She was found dead. The FBI has been called, but the Lieutenant on duty wants someone here to go hold the scene until they can get here to take over."

My head spins. *Julie? Dead?* "What? Are they sure? How—" Emily rolls over to face me.

"Yes, we are sure. I'm sorry to have to tell you this way."

I shake my head, as if to clear the fog that's rolling through my brain. How can she be dead? I saw her yesterday. "Shit. Yeah, ok. I'll be en route soon."

We hang up and I sit on the edge of the bed, numb. I feel Emily's hand move up and down my arm. "What is it?"

I turn to her, turning on the lamp. "I have to go to work. They found Sergeant Barton dead."

Her eyes widen. "What? That lady that I talked to?"

I nod. "Yeah. I can't believe this. I just saw her yesterday."

"I'm so sorry, wow." She pulls me into her arms before I can move to get up. I curl my arms under her back and let myself enjoy the feeling of her body against mine before I have to go face this awful thing.

"I'll be gone for a while. I probably won't be back before you wake up. Since it's already three in the morning, by the time I get done, it will be time to go to work."

She smooths my hair, running her fingers through it. "Okay. Be careful."

"I wish the damn alarm company hadn't pushed back our install. I don't like leaving you here." I mumble against her throat.

"Your gun is here. I'll be alright. I'll call you when I wake up."

I sit up and press my lips to hers. "Okay."

It's going to be a long day.

NOAH

I slink down in my seat as I watch Isaiah exit the apartment building and climb into his car. The bedroom light goes off just as he pulls out of the parking lot. I crack my knuckles. Now I just need to give her time to get back to sleep.

The dog barks once when I walk in. I stop short of kicking her. After a moment she realizes it's me, and then she dances around me. I ignore her. I shut the front door silently. I have to tell myself to still my breathing, which is coming faster now that I'm inside. My blood is running through my body like a freight train.

Creeping, I move into the bedroom. Moonlight comes through the slats on the blinds, falling across the bed, across her face. She's asleep on her back. She's wearing what looks like one of his t-shirts. Her red hair is fanned out on her pillow and her lips are parted in a deep breath. My heartbeat picks up. I haven't seen her in what feels like forever. *How can it be possible that she is more beautiful?*

On silent feet, I move to the side of the bed, and pull a capped syringe out of the front pocket of my sweatshirt. I've watched her enough to know what will and won't wake her. I flip on the dim lamp that sits on the night table beside the bed. Her arm hangs off the side of the bed, as if she's waiting for me and inviting me to take her. As I uncap the syringe, flicking it carefully to push the air out, I hold my breath. I've been waiting for this moment for so long. I push the needle into her arm. She moves. Her eyes fly open and a scream escapes her lips as she looks up into my face.

"No—"

I push the liquid into her arm and she starts to cry, but not for long. In a matter of moments, her eyes roll back and she goes limp; she's unconscious. I recap the needle and put it back into my pocket. Then I heave her up and over my shoulder, grabbing her phone from the night table.

No one sees me when I carry her to my car. I lay her gently into the back seat and cover her with a blanket. I don't want her to get chilly. It's cold outside tonight.

Leaning down, I touch my lips to hers for the first time. She tastes as sweet as I imagined she would. Tears blur my eyes as I linger, savoring the feeling.

"My angel, finally you are coming home."

CHAPTER 20

EMILY

I wake up with a start. The room is bright. Sunlight floods the room through huge windows. I scramble up. I'm naked. I'm not injured and nothing hurts. I'm in a huge, soft bed. It almost feels like I'm lying on feathers. I'm covered by a bright white thick comforter. Looking around, I realize that everything in the room is white: the furniture, the walls, the carpet.

Where am I?

Panic rolls into my body like a tidal wave as a brief memory flashes before my eyes: Noah was in my bedroom. I glance at my arm. There is a tiny bruise where he injected me with God knows what. On the table beside the bed is a carafe full of orange juice and a glass. There is a towel folded neatly on the dresser, which I assume is for me. I don't see anything else.

Am I locked in here? I get up. The carpet is soft and fluffy. I grab the towel for something to cover up with; it's oversized and wraps easily around my body.

Tears fill my eyes. *Is he going to kill me? Rape me?* Oh my God, Isaiah.

I try the closest door. It opens to a big bathroom.

I try another door. It opens to a closet full of clothes.

The third door opens. It's not locked. It leads out into a hallway. *What do I do?* Surely, he's here somewhere. *What if he's waiting for me to come out so he can...?*

I stifle a sob. Closing the door, I decide to search for my phone. As I'm opening drawer after drawer and finding nothing but clothes, I cry harder. I toss the items out of my way.

"Emily, you woke up." I hear my name and spin.

Noah stands in the doorway. He sees the mess and frowns, his brow wrinkling. "Angel, what are you doing? You can't make messes like this. I won't tolerate it."

I back up into a corner, sobbing and clutching the towel around my body. "What are you doing? Why am I here..." I hiccup.

He moves towards me and corners me. He touches my cheek with gentle fingers. "You are home, of course. Don't be afraid. I love you. This is all for you." He looks down into my face with tender, black eyes.

I can't breathe. I tremble, sickened by his fingers stroking my cheek. *Home?* I push away from him. "This isn't my home. I don't even know where I am. What the fuck are you doing?" I shout at him.

His wrinkles deepen on his forehead. "I know you are confused. It's alright. I'll get you cleaned up and show you around. All these clothes are yours. I'm going to give you the world, angel. I'm so happy that you are here. I've waited for so long for you."

"Get away from me. You're crazy!" I duck away from him, scooting to the other side of the room where he left the door open. I run out into a hallway; the floor changes from soft carpet to bright wood.

I feel a hand snatch me by the hair. I'm jerked back and pain shoots through my scalp. I yelp and try to turn and slap at him, but he's too strong. His arm goes around my waist and his hand covers my mouth. Tears run down my face and over his fingers. "Don't run from me. I don't want to have to hurt you, Emily. You must learn the rules and be a good girl." His hand tightens over my mouth. "Nod if you understand."

I nod, sobbing.

"You pick up all these clothes. Do you understand me?" He pulls me back into the bedroom, shutting the door. I nod again. He lets me go and I slink away from him, clutching the towel with one hand.

"I don't want to punish you, but I will if I must. I'll be watching you, Emily, while I get your bath ready."

I don't answer him. I stand, trying to memorize his face and my surroundings.

"Say yes sir to me. You hear me?" His eyes narrow.

I swallow. "Yes, sir."

His face relaxes. Then, to my horror, he pulls me against his body. "Thank you."

I burst into fresh tears. *Oh God, what am I in the middle of?* He leans in close, and for a horrible moment I think he's going to kiss me. Instead, he sniffs me. He lowers his head to my hair and my neck and smells me. "I love your scent."

I bite down a scream. *How does he know how I smell?* Of course he does, he's been in and out of my house for God knows how long.

"Now, do as I said and then meet me in the bath."

In the interest of saving my hide, possibly my life, I pick up the clothes and stuff them randomly back into the drawers.

The bathroom door looms before me. He leaves it open wide. Sitting on the edge of the bathtub, he pours in something that is making bubbles as the water fills. I stand trembling. I can't make myself move to the door. *Maybe this is my chance. Can I run out? How far would I get?*

I look outside. I see woods and a lake, but no sign of the city. I can't survive out there like this. With no idea of how far to run, or which direction, I'm stuck until I'm better prepared.

I imagine what Isaiah might say. I can hear his voice. *Fight. Survive. Do what you have to in order to make it home. Be smart. I'll find you.* I draw in a shaking breath. He has to find me.

"Emily, are you done?"

The overpowering scent of tea tree fills my nose. Turning, I see him standing with a towel draped over his arm. His bronze skin is in sharp contrast to the crisp white towel. I don't answer. I shuffle my feet and say a silent prayer to a God I haven't talked to in a long, long time.

The first thing I see is the tub. It's oversized and full of water so hot that steam is coming off it. It's got bubbles, and stinks of too much tea tree. There are soaps and shampoos and things on a shelf beside the tub. Noah smiles as if he's proud of himself.

The floor is strangely warm under my feet. Of course, this floor must be heated. I look down at a floor so black and shiny it's almost reflective. I glance around, but all I seem to be able to see is this tub. He wants me to get into it with him standing here I assume. Nausea rolls in my gut. I clench the towel tighter.

"Can you excuse me so I can bathe?" I ask softly, staring into the bubbles.

"Not this time. I have to make sure you're clean. You've been contaminated by that... man."

My Isaiah. I wonder if he knows I'm missing yet. I don't even know what time it is. Noah reaches out and pulls the towel off me. I keep my back to him. I can feel his eyes on me as tears spill from mine, struggling to cover my nudity with only my hands and arms. I hear his breathing in the quiet room.

"Get into the tub."

I stick a toe into the water and I quickly jerk it back. "It's too hot."

"It has to be to clean you properly. The tea tree will sanitize your skin. Get in."

He must not know how crazy he sounds. "Please, it will burn me. I'm afraid." I let my voice quiver, as I look over my shoulder at him.

He moves behind me and puts his hands on my bare shoulders. "It won't burn, angel. Get in."

I stick a foot in. It's so hot. Forcing both feet in, I'm crying, but unable to sit down. My feet, ankles, and calves are burning. My back still to him. "Please. It's too hot."

"Emily, you were bad. You let him touch you. You're dirty. I can't have you contaminate our home. Or me. Sit down. Now." There is a shard of anger in his tone.

I sit, slowly. I lower my body into damn near scalding water. I'm forced to turn, to fit into the tub. I lean back, but the bubbles don't cover my breasts. Noah gets down on his knees, and I cry silently. Nausea rolls over me again as I watch him pick up a bottle with French words on it. I'm filled with panic as he fills his hand with white, creamy liquid and moves to touch me.

Oh God, he's going to wash me.

When I jerk away from his touch, he scolds me with one look from his frightening eyes. I stop. He touches my left arm first. He lathers my arm with a purposeful yet slow touch, as if savoring it. He washes one arm at a time, and then my neck and shoulders. I blink away tears when his eyes move to my breasts. His hands are too soft for a man's. He rubs both breasts at the same time, slowly. His lips part and his eyes glaze. He drags his thumb over my nipples. He moves between my legs. I snap my thighs together and curl up.

"No, don't."

His eyes grow angry and his brow wrinkles. "What do you mean no?"

I scramble for an excuse. He thinks we are in love that much is clear. *What can I tell him to keep him off of me? Something that will fit into his twisted mind?*

"We aren't married. You can't." I blurt.

His pissed off face eases into a smile. "Married? Who said we have to be married? You weren't married to... him."

"Well... I'm all clean now... fresh... so... if I'm touched again by someone that I'm not married to, that will make me dirty again." I stumble over the fabrication.

He considers me, leaning over the tub and letting his hands dangle into the water. I hug my knees to cover my body.

"You want to stay clean and pure for me? For our wedding night?"

I can't look at him. I can't look at him.

I look up, meeting his eyes in a facade of sincerity. "Of course." I have to do whatever it takes to get home to Isaiah.

CHAPTER 21

ISAIAH

So many tears. When I get back to the police station everyone is crying. My phone has been blowing up with calls and texts all morning, everyone wanting to know what happened.

Every time I close my eyes, I see her laying there. Dead eyes, blue-gray, waxy skin, and her throat slit open.

There was no blood at the scene, telling us that she was killed elsewhere. She was found in her front yard. Whoever did this wasn't even trying to hide it. Seems he wanted her found.

I shake the images out of my head. I pass a lieutenant with damp eyes. He nods at me. I nod back. In all the years I've worked here, we've never had an officer die. She didn't die in the line of duty, but to be so brutally murdered and left naked out in the open like that is just as hard to take.

I walk into the Criminal Investigations Division door, slamming it behind me. I turn towards her office door. I told the FBI agent that I'd go through her office and recover anything that might be useful. The door isn't locked; it never is. Julie trusted everyone. I walk into her office and I catch the faint scent of her perfume. Painful numbness settles over me, and flashes of her dead body dance morbidly in my head as I move around to the back of the desk and sit where I saw her so many times before. I sit down and stare at piles of papers, folders, and post-it notes stuck all over her desk with her spidery handwriting. I toss anything in the file box that I think might be of use to the agent.

My phone jingles in my pocket. Pulling it out, I hope for Emily, but it's Billy. I hit ignore and dial Emily again. I called her earlier, but she didn't answer. No answer this time either. She must be busy at work. Telling myself she will call when she gets time, I dive into the desk with a heavy heart.

I come across a legal pad in her top drawer, and I lean back to peruse it. Noah's name, my name, and Emily's name all jump out at me. I scrunch up my forehead and read further. As I read through the notes, I realize this is from her conversation with Noah, about me "abusing" Emily. I almost toss it in the trash, knowing that she didn't do a real report. She was investigating this on the side.

Then I see her scratched note. "Noah took Emily's keys... he's not her boyfriend. He lied about being her boyfriend to get her keys." It's underlined three times. My heart slams against my ribs. *When did this happen? He got her keys? Why didn't she tell me?* Emily has my key too.

I jump up so fast the chair hits the wall, marking the sheetrock. I snap a picture of the legal pad with my phone and then close in on the note about the key, taking one more.

I call Emily again as I run down the hall towards the parking lot. No answer. My hands start to shake as I slam out the door and run across the parking lot to my personal vehicle. She would know better than to let me call this many times without answering.

I rush into the CVS, startling the cashier at the front. "Is Emily here?"

The old man blinks at me. "No, I don't think so."

I ask for the manager, he directs me to a display where a man is stacking cases of Sprite. "Is Emily here today?" I ask him.

"Um, no, not today." He goes back to his work.

I flash my badge at him. Now I have his attention. "Where is she?"

"She didn't show up for work. We called her and she didn't answer. Is she alright?"

I run a trembling hand over my face. "I don't know. If you hear from her, call me." I hand him a card with my office number on it after I scratch my personal cell on the back.

He nods. "I will."

I've never driven like this in my life. I run every light and hit almost eighty until I see my apartment complex come into view. In the parking lot I see that her car is still here.

Maybe she's sick.

Her dog jumps happily at my feet. "Emily, baby, are you here?" I call. My voice shakes.

No answer.

Room by room, I search. She's not here. I fall onto the couch, tears in my eyes. Maxie jumps into my lap.

I call her again. I leave a message.

Emily is missing.

DETECTIVE PATTERSON TUCKS a blonde curl behind her ear, staring down at the picture I sent her. She's standing in my apartment.

"So you just found out, right? Damn, I wonder why Julie didn't say anything." She mumbles, putting her phone back in sleep mode.

"I know she was friends with him, maybe she was worried about what she would find if she dug too far? Maybe she was afraid of him?" I offer, pacing.

Patterson watches me with sincere eyes. "We will find her, Isaiah. Her phone is still on, and it's not here. Maybe he has it. Let's get it located."

I nod, watching her call dispatch. She passes the number and the phone carrier info. "They are going to call me back. Let's go check her house, go to his house, his work, and talk to some people." She motions for me to follow her, surprising me.

"You're going to let me come with you?" Most wouldn't want someone in their investigation that's too close.

She doesn't look at me, just opens the front door. "Like me telling you to stay out of it is going to keep you here. Might as well be of use to me instead of getting in my way."

NOAH

I don't know if it's the right time to give her the ring. She's so damn skittish. When she gets out of the tub she backs away when I try to dry her off. She asks to be excused so that she can dress.

"Let me show you." I take her hand and drag her out of the bathroom. Her hand is hot. I lead her into the closet, which is almost as big as the bedroom itself. "These things are all yours." I motion to the right side of the closet. My things are on the left.

Lined with designer clothes, dresses, and a whole wall of shoes. She blinks, unspeaking. I pull out the drawers, showing her accessories—jewelry, handbags, belts, everything she could ever want. She seems to take it all in slowly.

"I did all this for you." I pull her toward a section of dresses. I want to see her in the white gown, but I will wait. I have so many special things planned. "Choose one."

She reaches up and selects a yellow dress. It's covered in small polka dots. Three quarter sleeves, soft cotton that will hug her curves. I lead her out the door to the dresser and open the panty drawer. I find the carefully selected items in a mess.

"Is this how you put these things back when I told you to clean this up?" I raise my voice.

She swallows, clutching the dress to her chest.

"There are rules. You understand? You must put things away properly. I won't tolerate mess or clutter. You won't be allowed to live the way you did before. I have a maid that will take care of the cleaning, but you must be neat. Do you understand me?"

She nods. "Yes."

I look down on her. "Yes, what?"

"Yes, sir. I'm sorry. I didn't know." Her voice trembles.

Trembling is good. It means respect. Respect means she will do as she's told. I nod, tossing the items out.

"Do it again, properly."

I watch her re-fold, carefully place each item back in its place. I open each drawer one by one and she does the same with each, crying silent tears the entire time.

"Can I please get dressed now?" She sniffles.

"Yes, then join me in the dining room for lunch." I leave her alone in the room.

I take my time setting out lunch for us on the elegant, black, glass table. I light candles, close the drapes to dim the room. I want it to be perfect. Our first meal together. The first of a lifetime. The phone in my pocket buzzes again. I check it.

Isaiah. He's calling Emily. I sigh, putting it back. I'm going to have to have her deal with this. I can't have him calling every few minutes. I considered ditching her phone, but I decided it might be handy to have around, so I've held onto it.

I hear the click of the door opening. Turning, I see her in the yellow dress. She's wearing a matching silver bracelet and necklace, earrings. She's put on makeup. Her heels click slowly on the floor.

I suck in a breath. "Emily, you look beautiful." The dress hugs her. Her hips sway as she walks, swishing the skirt around shapely legs. Her breasts heave in deep breaths as she approaches the table, avoiding eye contact.

"Thank you."

"I appreciate you dressing for me. Sit down." I pull out an upholstered chair. She sits and looks up at me with caution.

I can imagine having her up against the wall like I did Julie. Her skirt hitched up; her panting as I grip her hips. I take in a deep breath, moving to my seat trying to push the image away. There will be time for that later.

I can see she's uncomfortable. She shifts and seems to be unsure of what to do with her hands. Her food has a cover on it. A glass of wine sits to her right. Water beside that.

"Go ahead, eat." I prompt, uncovering my own plate.

She reveals the orange rosemary glazed salmon, asiago potato stacks, and mushrooms in red wine sauce. "Noah, can I ask where we are?" She carefully forks at the potato.

"We are at home, of course." I stare at her across the table. She shifts again, glancing up at me.

"This isn't my home. I don't know where I am. I live in Katy, Noah. I don't understand what's happening." Her voice is strong this time, not trembling. She looks up at me, meeting my eyes.

"This is your home now. You belong with me. I made this home just for you and I. Away from Houston. You don't need to work anymore. I'll take care of you. You have everything you need right here."

"But what about my friends, my... you can't keep me locked up. Not if you love me."

I meet a defiant gaze, bright brown eyes under even brighter red hair.

"What do you think this is, Emily? Why do you think you are here?" I set my fork down and lean my elbows on the table.

My question seems to have caught her off guard. She looks down, forking a mushroom and adding some salmon to the bite. "I don't know why I'm here."

"You called me and told me that you wanted to be my friend, didn't you?"

It takes a moment, but she nods.

"I told you that I love you when we talked that day, didn't I?"

Another nod.

"You are here to be with me. Live with me. So that we can share a life together. I know you are confused, but, in time, you will realize how much you love me and will see how well I can treat you. You'll want for nothing, I promise you. In time, you won't miss them."

She looks up with tears in her eyes. "Can't I please go home?"

Anger burns in my veins. I stand up, the chair falls behind me with a loud clatter. I move around the table and grab her by her hair, jerking her head back. She cries out and grips her fork like a weapon. I force her eyes to mine. "You are home. You will not be leaving me. I fought to get you here. I did bad things to get you here. I spent hundreds of thousands of dollars to make this home for you." The words come out in a hiss.

Tears flow from her eyes and her lips tremble. "Please don't hurt me."

"Don't make me hurt you. You will follow my rules, yes?"

"Yes, sir."

"You will not be a bad girl and make me punish you."

"Yes, sir."

I lean over and touch my lips to hers. They are salty and taste of the sauce on the mushrooms. She doesn't respond to me. I touch my tongue to her lips, but they don't part. I pull away. I grip her hair tighter and growl. "You will kiss me back when I kiss you."

She shakes her head, sobbing. I release her hair, only to give her the back of my hand. She falls in a tumble off the chair with a shout. She crawls backwards and holds her face. I crouch in front of her.

"See? I don't want to do these things, Emily. I adore you. You're my angel." I kiss her now puffy cheek. She stiffens. "You mustn't make me so angry. I've waited so long to kiss you properly."

I take the fork from her hand and toss it to the table. "Now, kiss me."

I watch her eyes, not moving. She wipes her face with both hands, drying her cheeks. My heart rate picks up when she leans forward and touches her lips to mine in a soft, warm kiss. Not stiff like the last one. She responds this time when I push her mouth open with my tongue, allowing me access. I groan. She tastes better than I imagined. Her tongue tangles with mine, as I hold her face in both hands and ravage the mouth that I've been waiting for.

I watch her wipe her mouth, taking in a breath. I knew it would be like this. It's going to be perfect.

I need her to do one more thing before things can move forward.

CHAPTER 22

EMILY

Noah helps me up off the floor. I want to spit the taste of him out of my mouth, but now I know better. There will be better ways to deal with him that that. I'll have to be smarter and do a bit of pretending. Maybe when he's drunk or asleep I'll be able to get out of here and find a phone. So yeah, I kissed him. I kissed him good. Now my damn face is throbbing and I feel like throwing up.

He looks down tenderly at me. "Are you ok? I'm sorry that happened."

I nod. "I'll be ok."

"Let's finish eating."

I make a show of cleaning my plate and drinking my wine. I follow him as told when he leads me to a large living area. This must be some sort of condo or townhouse. It's not massive at all, but he's decorated immaculately. The living room is black and white. He really seems to have a thing for white. I guess with his fixation on being clean, that makes sense. He sits down on a rich black suede couch and I'm told to sit beside him. He pulls something out of his pocket. I'm surprised to see that it's my phone.

I can see on the screen, seventeen missed calls from Isaiah.

God, no. My face twists in pain as I suck in a jagged breath.

Noah looks at me. "I need you to call him and end it."

I can't hide my tears this time. Not like with the kiss. "What? Can't we just... let him figure it out?"

"No. He needs to be told. Call him and tell him it's over. No games. He needs to know you are done."

I shake my head. A sob breaks out of my throat. "What if he doesn't believe me?"

Noah leans forward and pulls a hunting knife out of a sheath on his leg under his pants. "Make him believe it."

Something cold settles in my veins. I don't know if he means that blade for me or Isaiah. *Surely, by now, he has it figured out, right?* He never would've called me so many times if he wasn't scared to death.

He has to find me.

I take the phone, while eyeing the knife. It's got a bone handle he grips in his left hand. His other hand goes easily around my shoulder.

I hit the call back icon on the missed call screen, silently praying that he will somehow know where I am. Noah reaches over and puts the call on speaker.

"Emily... Emily, is that you?" His voice breaks.

A sob breaks out of my throat. Noah's hand squeezes the knife. His hand touches the back of my neck. "It's me. Um, I'm sorry for just up and leaving, but I need to—"

"Baby, are you okay? Just tell me if you are okay." His voice has tears in it.

God, he's crying for me. Fuck. I don't know how to go on.

"I'm not hurt, Isaiah. Listen to me for a minute, okay?"

He blows out a breath. "Whatever happens, whatever you are about to say to me, I have to tell you that I know, and I love you."

He knows? He knows what? Maybe he knows Noah has me? I leave the comment alone and struggle to find words that won't get me killed.

"I had to leave. Things were moving too fast. I guess I shouldn't have done it that way, but it's for the best I guess. I can't be with you anymore." The words choke me.

He's silent for a moment. Noah rubs the back of my neck. "You left all your stuff behind."

"I know."

"Is there someone else?" His voice is thick.

"Just take care of Maxie for me, okay? I'll come back for her later. I'm sorry to hurt you."

"Are you? You make me love you and then leave? Then you ask me to take care of your dog? Why should I?" he bites.

Noah nods his approval at me.

"Please, I... I don't know what else to say." The words break on sobs. Noah motions for me to wrap up the call.

"Yeah, I bet. But you are okay, right?"

"I'm not hurt Noah... I mean Isaiah. It's over. Goodbye." I hang up.

Noah narrows his eyes. I toss the phone to him. "It was an accident, really. I was just thinking about you and it slipped out."

He pockets my phone. On impulse, I crash into him and kiss him, to keep from getting stabbed or cut with that huge knife. He instantly melts into me, moaning. He must have dropped the knife, because I feel him move me into his lap and hold my ass in his hands as his erection starts to rub against my thigh.

God I'm going to throw up. I can't do this for long, but if I don't he will kill me. I just need to stay alive long enough for Isaiah to find me.

ISAIAH

No sign of her at her house. Not a surprise. The place was cleaned out and is ready to be put up for rent now.

As I sit in the passenger seat of Detective Patterson's Crown Victoria, I feel the tightness in my chest as we back out of the driveway. She's saying something to me, but I can't hear it. All I can think about is Emily's voice on the phone and her dropping Noah's name. I hope he isn't hurting her.

There isn't a doubt in my mind that he forced her to make that call.

I'm prepared to kill him if anything happens to her.

I'm ready to go to jail, should it come to that.

Patterson pats my arm. I glance over. She's about forty-five with short curly hair that's tucked behind her ears. She puts her sunglasses down over her eyes. "What are you thinking?"

"I'm thinking that she dumped me to save my life, or hers, I don't know which. I have no doubts that he forced her to do it. She dropped his name at the end on purpose."

The heater blows in my face on this cold January afternoon. "Would he hurt her?"

I shrug. "I don't know. He's clearly mentally ill. He thinks they are in love. It's possible that he won't want to. But it's also possible that he's sick enough to not realize what he is doing."

"Do you think she is smart enough to play along? Placate him until she can get a way out?"

I nod. "Without a doubt. She's smart. Are we headed back to the PD?"

"Yep. I need to get with dispatch and have her entered as a missing person, and check in on that phone information."

An hour later, we walk out of the PD. I flex my fingers in quiet rage. "What luck? The damn phone company is having some massive, computer upgrade today and we can't get her phone located until at least tomorrow, maybe longer," I grumble, slamming her car door.

Patterson starts the car. "Let's keep time moving by doing some good, old-fashioned, police work then. First stop... track down Noah."

We head to his shop, where they tell us he's not in today. He keeps his own hours and they never know when he is going to show up.

We go to his house, but his housekeeper won't let us in. She just says he's out of town on business and she can't let us in.

I suggest to Patterson that we go and see Caroline. She agrees and turns the car towards Houston.

The ride up in the elevator is silent. My eyes are burning with unshed tears. I don't want my coworker to see me bawling, even if it is justified. The urge to sink down to my knees and crumple into a shaking heap is almost more than I can swallow.

Patterson pats me on the back, eyeing me sideways. "Don't be a hero. It's okay to let it out."

I shake my head as the doors open. The familiar office door for Blue Line Enterprises looms. *Will Caroline be upfront with me this time?* I open the door for Patterson. She greets the receptionist with a smile and a flashed badge. We are asked to sit down and a hushed phone call is made to Caroline's office.

A moment later we are ushered in and offered coffee. Caroline is on the phone, but gestures for us to take a seat. Her eyes dart between the two of us.

The nervous receptionist brings our coffees and hurries out of the room.

"Hi, what can I do for you?" Caroline hangs up, avoiding eye contact with me.

"Caroline Davis, you know Emily Bronte, isn't that correct?" Patterson makes a show of setting a small recorder out on the desk.

"Yes." She glances at the device and then back up to Patterson. "Is something wrong?"

"She's missing. Last night Penrose here got called out to a murder, and Emily disappeared from her home sometime afterwards."

Caroline goes pale. She sits back, blinking slowly. "Missing? What? How?"

"That's what we are working on. Isaiah has told me about everything that's happened with you and her. Tell me, how are you involved with Noah Burrell?"

"Involved? He's my boss...my older brother... what's he got to do with anything?" Her voice fades, as does the rest of the color on her face.

"Tell me what you know about Noah's interactions with her."

She looks over at me. I cross my arms over my chest, watching her in silence. "Uh... I signed an agreement, I'm not supposed to talk about it."

Well, that's new. She didn't tell me that last time.

I lean forward, speaking for the first time since we entered the office in a low tone. "If he hurts her, you will be responsible if you know something. She was your friend. Doesn't that mean anything to you? Don't you have a heart in there somewhere?"

Tears fill her otherwise dim eyes. "Of course I do. I miss Emily. But he's my brother, he'd never..." Her voice quivers.

"Then why don't you help us find her? Noah is a dangerous man, Caroline. If you help us, maybe we can protect you."

Flashes of Julie suddenly enter my mind. She was friends with Noah. She was investigating our relationship. *What if he killed her?*

I fall back into my chair as the reality of this hits me. Fuck. *If he killed her so brutally, what would he do to Emily if he figures out she hates him?* I reach for my coffee and my hand is shaking so bad that I can't pick it up without spilling it. I look over at Patterson, who eyes me curiously.

"Caroline, did you happen to know Noah's friend, Julie Barton?" I ask. Patterson wrinkles her brow at me in confusion.

"No, I'm sorry I don't know many of his friends."

"Well, she's a Detective Sergeant in my department. She was found murdered early this morning. She was also investigating some claims that Noah made. I think that's an awfully big coincidence, don't you?"

"What? You think he... Hold on a damn minute. He was in here the other day making wild allegations about stalking, now this? After everything that Noah and this company have done for the police, you are harassing him? What's this about, really, money? I told him not to come back without a warrant. Do you have one?"

"Ma'am, we don't need a warrant to question you. This isn't Law and Order. We can detain you and take you to the police department if we need to. I suggest you stop tossing out these accusations and idle threats. Now, let's try this again. My investigation shows that Mr. Burrell has a pretty heavy history of some serious mental illness. Seems like he's functional, but has some problems. Can you tell us anything about that?"

"Am I under arrest?"

"No, not yet." I toss back.

She glares at me. "Then get out. I don't have to sit here and listen to this, or answer anything. You can't detain me if I'm not a suspect. I'm no fool."

Patterson leans forward and picks up her recorder, pockets it. She lays a card carefully on the desk, with a sweet smile. "Well, I'm sure we will be back, and next time it won't be so pleasant, I'm afraid. But if this is how you want it to go. We will get to the bottom of things, mark my words."

She turns to walk out, but I have to try one last time. "I just want Emily back safe, Caroline. Can you tell me where he is? Please?"

"No. And no, he didn't tell me where he went. Noah took some time off and left instructions that he shouldn't be bothered. His partner, Alex, is in charge while he's away."

I exchange a look with Patterson. "How long is he taking off?"

"I think about a month. He told everyone around here that he's getting married. Alex told me that he's had a girlfriend for a while now." She smiles at me. "Maybe Emily has been lying to you, maybe she opted for the better man." She grins this time, winking.

I crack my knuckles to hide the tremors in my hands. He thinks he's going to marry Emily. Shit. If marrying him until I can find them is what it takes, then I hope she does it to stay alive. This guy might be a killer. Annulling a marriage is a hell of a lot easier than... the unthinkable.

"You ever met his girlfriend?" Patterson jumps in.

"No, no one has that I know of. Alex teased him about it."

"Don't you think that is strange?"

"No, I don't. He's just private. He just likes to keep his home and work separated."

"That's a possibility I suppose. But, from what I've seen, most people like to show off their loved ones. Especially if they care enough about them to marry them."

"That's not always the case." She crosses her arms over her chest.

"Do you have an emergency number for him?"

My heart rate picks up. Please say yes. "You must be joking." Caroline lets out a long laugh.

"Can you give me Alex's name and phone, and where I can go see him?"

"Goodbye, detectives."

I pull my phone out of my pocket, and I hand her my card. She ignores it. I let it drop on the desk.

Out in the hall way, I suddenly realize that I left my phone behind. A moment later, when I walk into Caroline's office, I find her crying.

"What are you doing here?" She bolts up, sniffling.

"I left my phone. Caroline, look," I walk around and sit on her desk, looking down into her eyes. "Whatever you have going on with

Noah, I don't care. I just want Emily back home. I love her. I know that you can help me more than you are letting on. I can help you get out of whatever deal you think that he has you tied into."

Fresh tears roll from her overly made up eyes. I can tell she's afraid to answer me, so I keep talking.

"I just want her back. I want her safe and with me. Can't you understand that? What if it was Gary? Being stalked by some crazed woman that might hurt him?"

She nods. "I understand. You really do love her?"

Strange how her entire mood changed in the span of a few minutes. My voice cracks on a lump forming in my throat. "I do. I don't even know if she realizes how much I love her. Please, Caroline. I need your help."

A moment passes between us. She wipes her eyes. I choke on tears, struggling to keep them at bay.

"Look, I really don't know anything. Noah and I aren't really that close. We are so far apart in age, by the time I was born he was already graduating high school and ready to go off to college. He might have issues, but he's harmless."

Big eyes looking up at me, sniffling, biting her lip and glancing away. The body language tells me that she's serious, but the bells going off in my head tells me that there is something wrong with this. Something big, but I'll be damned if I know what it is. I swallow the feeling, trying to focus on the fact that I need anything I can get to get Emily back home safe, and this guy away from her. "He hasn't called you since he left?"

"No, he went off the grid. He does that from time to time. It helps him settle his mind."

I nod. Chewing on my lip for a moment as I think on what she's told me.

"This is between us. If he calls you, call me day or night. Got it?"

I pass her my personal number, the one not on my card. She takes it. "Okay."

"Can I trust you to call me?"

"Yes." *We will see.*

"Whatever he wants, play along. Tell him you will do it, and then call me and tell me what's going on."

Caroline meets my eyes. "Alright. I'm so sorry, Isaiah. I hope you find her."

"Me too."

CHAPTER 23

NOAH

Her legs spread over my hips, she lets me slide my hands up her skirt, the bare skin of her thighs burning my hands almost as much as they are burning my erection as it sits between them. My tongue is deep in her mouth, and her hands are on my shoulders. She needed to be free of him to open herself up to me.

I knew she loved me and wanted me. I squeeze her ass in both hands. She's wearing one of the thongs I got her. I got her nothing else. I can't wait to see her ass in them. The bare skin makes me groan as I slide my palms over it, tucking my fingers into the silky waist band.

I sink my teeth into her lip with a groan. The sharp taste of blood and the cry of pain startles me. She scrambles off my lap.

"You bit me!" she accuses, wiping the blood from her lips.

I try to catch my breath. "I got excited. Are you alright?"

She doesn't meet my eyes. I get up and get a cloth napkin from the lunch table and touch it to her lip. Still she doesn't make eye contact. Her lip is already bruising as I touch it with the cloth. The sight of her mouth makes me want it again.

"I'm sorry, I didn't mean to hurt you. I like rough sex," I confess, softly. "I got carried away."

Her eyes move up for a fleeting moment. I toss the cloth down on the coffee table.

"Rough sex? I don't enjoy being hurt."

Her voice is trembling. There is fear in her eyes. Fear. Respect. Fear. Respect. They are the same. I smile and run a hand over her cheek.

"When we are married, I think that you will grow into it. I'll be gentle with you, angel."

God I can almost feel it, being deep inside her. Her warmth engulfing me, her breathy moans gasping my name.

She doesn't answer me. "Angel, do you want to marry me?" I ask quietly.

Soft, respectful brown eyes float up to meet mine. She licks her now puffy lower lip. "Are you asking me?" There are tears in her voice.

I drop to one knee and pull out the Tiffany engagement ring I've had for months now. It's a two carat ring with a halo of smaller diamonds around it, and down the band.

"Will you marry me? I love you and want everything I have to be yours. I want to shower you with everything you can ever want and love you forever."

She backs up a step. I reach and slide the ring onto her finger. Tears fill my eyes. I've dreamed of this moment, every day, every night-the moment that I finally make her mine. Her- in my bed, as my wife- Our wedding night.

"Isn't it a bit soon? We just... I don't even... it's..." She fumbles. She gapes at the ring on her finger.

I grab her hips and stare up at her. "Does that matter? When it's right, it's right. We will have all our lives to answer all those questions together."

My heart slams against my ribs. *Is she going to say no?* She can't say no to me.

"Can I have some time to... I just need to get used to all this."

I stand up with a sigh. "I guess so. Do one thing for me while I wait."

She stares up at me, waiting.

"Tell me you love me."

Her eyes drift over to the hunting knife on the table. I reach over and pick it up, walking towards the hallway to put it away. She hesitates for too long. I turn to face her, gripping the knife that I opened Julie's throat with in my right hand.

"I'm waiting."

She blinks at me. "I love you."

The words calm my soul. I take a deep cleansing breath, as if I can breathe her voice into my lungs like clean ocean air. I shove the knife into my belt and cross the gap between in two long strides, grabbing her face in my hands and turning it up towards mine. She blinks away tears and her puffy lip trembles.

"Doesn't it feel better to be honest with yourself? To let it out?" I ask, softly.

"Yes."

"Good girl. I'm going to make you so happy, my angel. So happy." I bend and touch my lips to hers. She stiffens at first, but then breathes in and accepts my lips.

I knew all I needed to do was remove the obstacles. Now she's mine.

EMILY

The knife. All I can think about is that huge, fucking knife hanging on his belt. He has his mouth on mine and I swallow down my nausea as he invades me with his disgusting tongue.

I wonder how fast he is. *Can I get my hands on that knife and... can I actually stab someone?* I blink back tears. He's bigger than me. Not as big as Isaiah, but still bigger. He's a lot older too. *He has to sleep eventually, right?* Maybe I can get out then.

But the door has an alarm on it. *How fast can I run? Is there a car outside? Where are the keys?*

He pulls away from me with a sickening smile. "I'm going to put this away. I'll be right back. I still need to show you around. I need to show you everything I've made for you here."

I nod. I can't force a smile onto my lips. He doesn't seem to notice.

After a moment he comes back and takes my hand. I'm glad for this tour, since I have no idea where I am. Maybe he will take me outside too.

He takes me from room to room. The living room and dining room, just off a big galley style kitchen, are open floor plan. It's a nice size, but not huge. It is decorated immaculately, of course. He passes the room I woke up in and shows me a room with a keypad lock on the door. He announces it as his office as he unlocks the door, blocking the code from my vision with his body. The room is dark with a big desk in it. Behind it is a wall lined with books, which are probably for decoration. It's neat. There's virtually nothing on the desktop. Everything in this house smells like cleaner. As we exit the study, I realize that there are no other rooms and I panic. He grips my hand with a smile.

"Where is your bedroom?" I ask, my voice high.

He frowns at me. "What do you mean? Why would I have my own bedroom? The room you woke up in is our bedroom, not yours. I have clothes in the closet beside yours. We are together. We share. Don't you want to share?"

My mouth opens and closes like a goldfish. My palms start to sweat. He expects me to sleep with him in the same bed.

I think I'm going to throw up. Holy God.

The knife. Remember the knife. My mind is blank, other than this one thought playing over and over. Effectively numbing me from paralyzing terror so that I can think semi-rationally. He's insane. He's dangerous and delusional. When he goes to sleep, maybe I can find some meds and drug him or something. There has to be a way to get out of here. *I have to find a way out of here.*

"I just didn't know. I woke up alone, so—"

Something akin to relief smooths out the wrinkles on his forehead. "You won't ever wake up alone again, Emily." He leads me towards the front door. "Let me show you the outside."

We step out onto a long porch. Turns out, this is a house. The exterior is covered in what looks like redwood slats and stone. There are no neighbors in sight. The house is mostly surrounded by woods. There is a lake on one side, with a dock and a little boat tied up. There is a detached garage; its door is closed so I can't see the car.

Around back there is a big, covered, redwood deck with a sunken fire pit surrounded by outdoor couches. There is also a steel, outdoor kitchen. It really is beautiful, but I hate it. I hate it with everything that I am because he's taken me from Isaiah.

I can't fight the tears this time. I am flooded with memories of my love. The memory of the smile on his face and the sound of my name on his lips. The memory of how he liked to lay between my legs after sex and rest his head on my bare breast and purr in the afterglow. The memory of his birthday and how he told me he loves me.

Tears roll down my face and sobs wrack me as I pull away from Noah and fall to my knees. *If I beg, would he let me go?*

I fell in love so fast. I've never known anything like the feelings that Isaiah stirs up inside me. *What if I never see him again? What if he can't find me? What if he believed me when I broke up with him and didn't pick up on my hint?*

I feel hands on my shoulders and I slap at them. I don't want Noah to touch me. I don't want him to ruin my memories of Isaiah by touching me when I'm thinking of him.

Anger boils within me. My mind tells me to keep quiet or he will hit me. If I confess my hate he might even kill me. I have to keep my mouth shut. So I just sob. Nausea lurches me forward and I vomit all over the deck. Up comes the fancy salmon and mushrooms that I forced myself to eat.

I fall back on my ass, and cry as he crouches in front of me. I cover my face with my hands. I hear his voice. "What is wrong with you?"

I uncover my face, and the words come out before I can think to stop them. "Please, will you let me go home? I—"

His black eyes go cold and a chill runs down my spine. "This is your home. Emily, look at me." He grips my chin too tightly and jerks my face up. "Remember one thing: I will kill you before I let you go. I bought this house for you, for us. You are mine now. Don't forget that, and don't ask me again." His voice is hard. If not for the fact that I just barfed, I think I'd be sick again. The dead look in his scary eyes tells me that he probably would kill me before he ever let me go.

"Now get up and clean up this mess." He jerks his head in the direction of a water hose.

Bedtime. This is what I've been dreading all day. I've spend every moment with him today. Now, he's crossing the room wearing silky, black pajama pants and no shirt. Of course, that's because he gave me the matching shirt to sleep in. After my shower, I searched high and low for a pair of regular panties. There's nothing but skimpy thongs in the drawer though. The idea of sleeping next to him with just a thong between me and him terrifies me. I know I won't be sleeping. I'll have to fake it. Maybe when he goes to sleep I can look around.

Noah gazes at me with a soft look that I want to look away from. He lays down beside me. My heart starts to beat hard. *What if he tries to touch me? What if he wants sex? What if he won't wait, like we talked about in the tub today? Would he rape me?*

My only hope is knowing that he is convinced that he loves me. If I can convince him that I love him and want to wait, maybe he will. Problem is, I'm so scared of him that I'm having a hell of a hard time pretending to love him.

I cringe inside when he reaches over and touches my hair. Leaning up on his elbow, he watches my lips as he traces them with the same finger.

"My angel, have you thought more about my proposal?"

I forgot all about it. Hard to believe with this rock on my finger, but I did. If I say yes, he's sure to believe me, right? I force my eyes to his, and silently tell myself not to bite his finger.

"I have. Ask me again."

He smiles at me. "Will you marry me?"

"Yes."

A grin breaks his face open. I force a smile as he takes my face in his hand.

"I love you."

"I love you, too."

He kisses me. It is like a deep invasion. I'm sure he thinks he's being sensual and sexy, but it makes me want to cry. I kiss him back with as much enthusiasm as I can muster. I feel his hand on my thigh, and then drifting up to my hip. He pulls my body into his. His breathing sharpens and his mouth moves to my throat.

"Do you know how happy I am to have you in my bed?" He pants against my skin. He's managed to pop two buttons open, pressing hot lips to the exposed cleavage. His tongue darting over my skin.

My heart feels like it's going to explode as I fight the urge to scramble away from him. If I want to live, I have to pretend that I want this too. I have to be disappointed when I tell him to stop. He palms my breast in his hand, groaning.

"Emily, I want you."

He climbs on top of me, his weight pressing me into the bed. Nothing between me and his arousal but this satin as he presses it between my thighs. He jerks my shirt up. "God, you're beautiful."

I let him stare at my body. He's already seen it anyway.

"It will be better on our wedding night."

He blows out a breath, leaning over and kissing my stomach. "Are you really going to make me wait? I'll be jerking off in the bathroom every day." He laughs, watching my face as he drags his mouth up between my breasts.

I suck in a breath, trying to appear turned on. I bite my lip and wiggle under him. I touch biceps that need to be in the gym.

"I'm sorry. But won't it be better when I'm all yours, forever?"

He smiles at me and crashes into my lips. "Do you like these panties?" He pops the waistband playfully.

I nod. "They are lovely."

"You look sexy in them." He kisses me again.

"I'm glad you like it."

We end up making out for a while. He lays on top of me. I let him kiss me and run his hands over my body. He laughs when I tease him and slap his hands away from my panties. He's buying it. He's having a good time. I see it in the sparkle in his black eyes. He tells me over and over how good I feel, how much he loves touching me, and how it turns him on.

At some point, he gets up and disappears into the bathroom. I jerk my shirt down, turn the lamp off, and curl up under the blanket. Maybe if he takes long enough he'll believe I've gone to sleep.

I close my eyes and slow my breathing. Laying on my side, I hear him come out. I feel him get into bed and press up against me. His hand is on my ass, rubbing it, but I don't budge. His face is in the back of my neck. He eventually snakes his hand around and cups a breast, relaxing against me.

I wait what feels like hours. When I finally hear soft snores coming from him, I get up. If he wakes, I plan to tell him I got hungry or had to pee or something. He rolls onto his back, still snoring, as I slip out of his grip.

Now, to find that phone. Isaiah must be worried sick. I saw Noah empty his pockets into the top, right hand drawer.

On tiptoe, I move. I slide the drawer open and will my eyes to see in the dark. I can't quite make anything out. I reach in and feel around. I feel a wallet and a money clip. No keys, damn it. He must have them hidden. Then I feel it, a phone. I push a button and see it's mine, right beside his. Mine is still holding a charge. I take it and tiptoe out of the room.

ISAIAH

I lay in bed staring at Emily's empty pillow. Burying my face in it to catch the scent of her shampoo, I feel tears well up in my eyes as my phone notifies me of a text.

I grab it, thinking maybe Patterson found something. Then I laugh. It's almost midnight.

My heart explodes at Emily's name on my screen.

Isaiah, are you there? I don't know where I am, he won't tell me. I'm not hurt, but he wants me to marry him. We are in this little house and seems like we are in the woods by a lake. I don't see anything I recognize. I'm scared to call. He's asleep. Are you there? Please be awake.

What if it's him? I text back with shaking hands.

Who is this?"

It's me, baby. Emily. He's asleep. I found the phone.

Fuck... are you ok? Has he hurt you? Call 911.

I can't tell them where I am.

Can you call me?

I'm scared to. I don't want to wake him up. I don't know where he's keeping his car keys either. He hasn't hurt me. Can't you find me?"

Tears fall, and my shoulders shake. She's alive. *I'm trying. We talked to a lot of people today, but no one could tell us where he went. He said he was going off to get married. I'm going to find you. Tell me everything about where you are.*

She shoots off a long text describing everything about the place and the remote surroundings.

Then I get an idea. *Send a text to 911. Just tell them the truth, that you don't know where you are, and ask them what city or county that your text reached. Every city has its own 911. It will tell me where to start looking if they can't find you.*

She agrees. Tells me she loves me in case she doesn't get back to me.

I'm pacing fifteen minutes later, wondering if she got caught or the battery died. I can't text her unless she texts me first, knowing she would clear the messages so he doesn't find out if he catches her.

I'm back. Ellis County.

I take in a breath. *That's just south of Dallas County. What did they say?*

They are going to have a deputy search the area. She said without an address it's the best they can do. I told them my name. She said I'm missing.

We will find you, I promise. I'll be getting in the car as soon as I hang up and heading to Ellis County to find you. I can visit the county clerk's office in the morning and request his records, maybe get an address for him.

You have to hurry. He thinks we are engaged. He got me a ring. I'm scared he's going to want to go to Vegas soon. I told him I won't sleep with him unless we are married. I was trying to keep him off me without making him angry.

I'm shaking so bad that I can't hardly text her back. She's smart. I'm going to kill this bastard when I get my hands on him.

Good thinking. I love you so much, baby. Do what you have to, stay alive. I'm coming.

What do I do if he wants to go to Vegas? If you don't get here in time?

Marry him if you have to. We can get that annulled. I'll find this place. If you are gone when I get there, I'll head to Vegas. If you can, leave me a message. I'll break into the place if you're not there. I'm coming for you baby. Look for an opportunity to run away.

Please hurry. If I have to marry him, he'll expect me to have sex with him. I'm scared he'll really hurt me when I reject him. I just heard a noise, I have to go. Please hurry.

I stare at my phone for a full thirty seconds before my head comes back to me. Then I roar and put my fist through the sheetrock in my bedroom wall. If he touches her, if he hurts her... I just can't think about it.

I have to keep my head clear. I can't let myself think about that right now. I can't find them if I'm focused on the wrong thing. Blood drips from my knuckles as I toss my phone onto the bed.

Time for a road trip.

CHAPTER 24
NOAH

I roll over in bed and Emily isn't beside me. A surge of panic bubbles within my chest. My first thought is to remember that my car keys are locked securely in my office. There is a code lock on the door and a second key lock on the drawer.

Maybe she got thirsty. I get up and walk slowly into the living room, finding her in the kitchen. She's over the sink with a glass of water. The black, silk top hangs to her knees, rolled up cuffs halfway up her arms. The sight of her bare legs and mussed hair makes me grin. Judging by last night she will love what I have in store today. She sees me and sets down the glass.

"I woke up thirsty."

"Get enough water? Come back to bed." I tug on her sleeve.

She smiles a small smile at me, nodding.

After a trip to the bathroom, I walk into the bedroom and see her curled up in the dark under the blankets. Being cautious, I check my drawer. Both phones in place. Blowing out a breath of relief, I close the drawer quietly and get back into bed.

After waking, I make coffee and I enter my office. I woke up before Emily, which gives me time to get some work done. I open my email and start to answer one after the other. Some I refer to Alex, who is running the show while I'm away. Others I refer to district managers like Caroline.

I blow out a breath. That's done. Now to set up my plans for today. I open up the internet and proceed to book us a flight to Las Vegas for this afternoon. Afterwards, I get up and pack two bags for us, sure to be careful with the slinky white gown I've chosen for Emily. She sleeps in the middle of the bed, laying on her stomach. The curtains are drawn as I watch her from inside the closet, tossing clothes for both of us into the suitcases.

She's finally going to be mine. By tonight, I'll be married to her and inside her, and she's going to beg for me to do it again and again.

God, I can't wait.

ISAIAH

It's a long drive. Even longer when you leave in the middle of the night and you haven't slept a wink. I down the last of my coffee with a double shot of espresso as I pull into the parking lot of the Ellis County Courthouse. I called the clerk from the road. She was more than happy to pull the files for me and put my name on them when I did a bit of flirting with her.

I walk into the county clerk's office. It's empty accept for the brunette behind the desk. She's staring at a computer screen through glasses. Looks to be in her thirties. The sound of the door draws her attention up. Her eyes drift over me and a smile hits her face.

"Hi, are you Abby?" I grin, leaning casually on the counter. I lift my sunglasses, placing them on my head and I meet brown eyes.

"Yes, I am. Can I help you?"

"Well, you've already been so helpful. Frankly, I'm a bit hurt that you don't remember me. We spoke on the phone this morning."

Recognition hits her face and a shy grin pulls her lips up. "Oh, you must be Detective Penrose?"

I stick out my hand. "Guilty. Call me Isaiah." I wink.

She takes my hand, a blush coming to her cheeks. "How could I forget? Isaiah." She giggles.

I watch her pull a manila folder off of her desk and open it. "Well, I'm glad that I'm memorable."

She blushes again. Her gaze drifts over my face, down my chest, and back up. I'm wearing a plain blue t-shirt with POLICE across the front. My gun belt, with my badge hanging off the side. When I find Emily, I want to be clearly marked as a cop.

She slides a single page report across the desk to me. "Is this what you were looking for?"

I take it. It's got one address on it. Not being familiar with this county, I'll have to Google it. I look up at her with a broad grin.

"It is. Thanks, beautiful. Do I need to sign something?"

She shakes her head. "No, don't worry about it. It's open records anyway. How long are you in town?"

I fold the paper carefully. "Just today. This investigation is moving fast, sweetheart. Thanks again, you don't know how much you've helped."

I walk backwards towards the door. She gives me a "your welcome" and I head back to the car.

My phone tells me it's one fifteen. Google tells me that the drive to this address will be about forty-five minutes. My heart rate picks up speed and my mouth goes dry at the thought of finally finding her.

The drive takes a little longer, thanks to a big accident on the freeway. I sit, immobile for close to thirty minutes before traffic finally starts to crawl again. As a police officer, you would think that I would show patience, understanding the process of accident investigation, closing down a busy street, and getting vehicles moved off the roadway. Normally, maybe so.

Not today.

I slam my fist on the wheel and let a stream of filthy words break from my lips. When every moment counts, when I'm so close I can taste it, I get this crap.

My phone rings. I glance over, hoping for Emily. It's Patterson. I left her a somewhat garbled message at four am this morning as I was gathering up my stuff to leave.

"Hello."

"What in the hell are you doing? Your message..."

I proceed to tell her the whole story. Emily's text messages, where I am, and the information I got from the county clerk.

Patterson sighs loudly. "You better go over there with cops, Isaiah. Don't get yourself killed."

"I don't have a warrant. I don't need cops to knock on a door."

"You need back up."

"I'm fine. If I need it, I'll call, I promise. I don't even know if this is where she is. He might have her somewhere else."

"I understand your reasoning but losing one cop this week is enough. We don't want to lose another one. And on that note, I talked to Agent Barker about all the stuff you told me. He's going to look into Noah and his relationship with Julie. He seemed to be very interested."

"Good. I hope he meant it. I'll let you know what happens, ok?"

"Alright. Bye."

I hang up and toss the phone aside. I'll find her, it it's the last thing I ever do.

The address is harder to find than I expected. Old, unnamed roads are to blame. Finally, I pull into a modern yet somehow still country-style home in the woods, on a lake. Just like she said. No cars in the driveway.

My heart is racing as I circle the house, peeking in windows. No one is here. I check the doors, but they are locked. With a dry mouth and trembling hand, I break a window and hesitate before gaining entry, making sure that no one is home.

I fly from room to room, searching for signs of Emily, as an alarm blares in my ears. When I come to the bathroom, inside an all-white bedroom, I'm greeted with a message in lipstick on the mirror with a smiley face: Las Vegas here we come.

Damn she is smart. He would see that and think she's excited. I'm on the phone with the airline before I'm out the front door.

CHAPTER 25

EMILY

Noah keeps asking the flight attendant for drinks. I shake my head, but he laughs and ignores me, pushing yet another glass of expensive champagne at me. I sip on glass number four.

"Can I have some water? I don't want to be drunk."

"Of course. Anything for my bride. When we get there, I'll buy you dinner and then we can find a chapel."

I nod. If Isaiah doesn't show up, I'm going to want to be drunk later.

I can only hope that he found the house and saw my message. I was afraid Noah was going to go berserk, but he came out of the bathroom with a smirk. He pulled me tight against him and kissed me. As horrible as that moment was, I was happy. My message was left for Isaiah to find.

As the buzz from the champagne hits me, the only word I can think of to describe all of this is surreal. Weeks ago, I thought this guy was just an annoying customer. Now he's kidnapped me, I'm stuck on a plane with him, and I'm pretending to be excited about marrying him.

What if I have to marry him? What's he going to do to me if I refuse him his wedding night? I down another glass of champagne that's been set in front of me. I glance over and find Noah is watching me with a crooked smile.

"Where do you want to go for the honeymoon?" he asks me in a low voice, leaning close.

I didn't even think about that. Shit. He's going to want to take me on a honeymoon. He thinks all this is real and we are in love and I'm thrilled. He'd lose his mind if I told him the truth; that is, if he hadn't already lost it.

I shrug. "I have no idea. I've never been much for traveling. What hotel are we staying in?"

"The Bellagio. The Tower Suite. Only the best for my angel on her wedding night."

My eyebrows go up. "Generous of you."

He chuckles. "It's nothing. You'll see, you will have the best of everything now. You make me very happy, Emily. I love you very much."

I swallow a lump in my throat. I suddenly miss Isaiah so much it hurts. It's only been a couple of days, but these have been two of the longest days of my life.

I know what he's expecting. I blink and smile. "I love you too. I'm sure it will be amazing. Can you excuse me? I need to visit the ladies room."

He shifts, allowing me access to the aisle. I blow out a breath. I feel his eyes on me as I walk down the aisle and behind the curtain that divides the restroom area from the cabin. Pushing forward, through another curtain, I find myself in the kitchen area.

Ask for help. Grab someone and scream bloody murder. Maybe the pilot can help me, right? *But what if they don't believe me? He could snap my neck in a second. What if he got a weapon past security? It happens all the time. I can't put a whole plane full of people at risk; what if he's crazy enough to bring the whole damn plane down?* Knowing I only have a moment to decide, my thoughts become a jumbled mess, leaving me grasping. I don't know what to do.

"Pardon me, may I help you?" a young, friendly flight attendant chirps.

I smile. "My phone battery died and I need to text my boyfriend. He's freaking out about being alone with our baby for the first time. May I borrow yours to send him one text? Please?"

She smiles and shoots me a look of sympathy. "Oh, of course. I understand. My husband was all thumbs with our baby just last year." She hands me a large, Samsung phone.

I take it, entering Isaiah's number from a memory that I'm surprised still works. I text him. *Texting from a flight attendant phone. Headed to Vegas, Bellagio, Tower Suite. I'm not hurt.*

He texts me back a second later. *Got it babe. I'm on my way. Hold on tight.*

Relief wraps around me like sunshine on a warm day. I delete the messages and hand the phone back to her with a smile and a profuse thank you.

I'm so happy that I managed to get a text off that I almost forget to stop and use the bathroom. When I get back to my seat, Noah is smiling and there is a bottle of water waiting for me.

The happiness from my brief contact with Isaiah is short-lived. I manage to struggle through the small talk on the three hour flight with Noah, avoiding talking about the future whenever possible.

We catch a cab from the airport. I know that it won't be long before we are married and I'm either being killed or raped. I watch the cars go by. Is this the end for me? Will anyone get here in time to help me? Or should I be scratching my will out on a note pad in the hotel bathroom? We pull into the hotel parking lot and I feel nauseated. When we walk inside, I scan the lobby. There is no sign of any help, no police, nothing.

As Noah presents a credit card to a smiley man behind the desk, I kick at the pattern in the carpet. Isaiah knows where we are staying. He will be here sometime tonight, surely. I have to hold onto this hope, the other option is just too crippling to allow into my mind. This isn't reality; it can't be. But, as Noah's hot hand curls around mine once more, I know that it is reality. My reality.

I look towards the door and contemplate making a run for it. It's too crowded. I can't risk being stopped by someone, and then beaten in the room upstairs. It's best to just wait, I guess. If I see an opportunity to run, I will, but this isn't it.

The suite is the size of an apartment. I gape as I walk in front of Noah. He insisted that I go first. I'm sure he wants to keep his eyes on me now that I'm not contained on an airplane. The entry way is spectacular. Polished marble leads into a large sitting area, which is the size of a full living room. To the right, there is a wet bar. The far wall is lined with windows, which gives us a grand view of the strip. The carpet is thick and plush, even under my Nike's.

Noah calls to me and ushers me into the bedroom. I stop in the doorway with heart palpitations when my eyes fall on that bed. I try not to look at him, but my eyes are drawn to him when he lifts the suitcase to the bed. He looks up at me as he unzips the case with a smile of anticipation in his eyes.

God, where is Isaiah.

I watch, mute, as he pulls a white box out of the suitcase. He motions for me to come to him. "This is for you. I want you to wear this for me."

I hesitate as if there is a snake inside the box. I sigh, louder than I intend, and I open the box. Inside I find my wedding dress. The dress is white satin or silk, I'm not sure which, form fitting, with a deep V, backless, and has spaghetti straps. Inside the box is also a sparkly, barely-there thong. He pulls strappy silver shoes out of the suitcase and hands them to me.

I want to throw the shoes and the dress at him and run out the door. I don't want to marry him. But I'm terrified. He's holding me prisoner. I know that he has that huge knife somewhere. I don't know how he got it past airport security. He's also fully demonstrated that he has no problem "punishing" me if I'm "bad." He hit me once, showed me that damn knife, and he's too big for me to fight off on my own.

I look up at him and see distinct lust on his face.

"Do you like it? I saw it and knew that you would look amazing. I've been saving it."

Bile rises in my throat. I swallow it back down as the fabric slips between my fingers back into the box. "Thank you. I'll go get changed."

I take the box and the shoes and vanish into the bathroom. It's huge. I'm surrounded by granite and marble and shades of tan and brown. There is a big bathtub and a massive shower. The towels are plush and thick. I don't give one hot damn about any of it. Tears fill my eyes as I sit down on the edge of the bathtub. I try to regain my composure. I don't want him to know that I was crying.

My hands are shaking. I look into my reflection's brown eyes. I'm pale. My red hair is stark against the unusual whiteness of my skin. Carefully, I pull off my clothes. The designer jeans. The yellow blouse. My bra and panties.

I put on this obscene thong. It doesn't even really cover anything. I step carefully into the dress, seriously thinking for a moment about "accidentally" ripping it, but, of course, I don't. I don't know what might set him off. I'd hate to already be dead when Isaiah or the police finally make it here. The material is cold against my skin. I can't wear a bra with a dress like this. The cloth outlines every curve of my breast. The deep v dips well below my breast. I feel naked. It hugs me and leaves almost nothing to the imagination. The back is so low my ass almost comes out the top. I put on the shoes and look at my reflection. I roll my eyes. I feel like a hooker.

There is a gentle knock on the bathroom door. His voice comes through muffled. "Are you alright?"

No, I'm not even close to alright. "Yes. I'm coming."

The look on his face when I open the door is just what I was afraid it would be: pure sex. It's a look that tells me he wants nothing more than to fuck me, in this dress, right now. My first instinct is to back away, but I can't.

He's got his arm around my waist and he pulls me tight against his body. I fight a cringe as his lips find my ear and his breathe is on my neck. "You look sexy."

I feel his lips on my jawline and I blink back tears. I hate this. I hate him. I want my life back.

I'm so miserable and scared that when he takes me out for dinner, I'm not even paying attention to where we end up. All I know is it's fancy, and men keep looking at me. I eat slowly, dreading what's coming. Trying to kill the time between this moment and the altar, I order dessert, and he watches me with a smile as I force it into my sick stomach.

When I can't think of anything else to stall with, I ask to go to the bathroom. I'm planning to run out while he's paying. But he follows me to the bathroom. When I come out he's leaning against the opposite wall with his hands in his trouser pockets. He keeps a hand on me for the rest of the night. I assume he's afraid I'm going to run. Smart man.

Before I know it, we are in the cab ride on the way to the chapel.

At the altar, an old man reads out of a book. He puts the ring on my finger, and then I do the same to him. I promise to love, cherish, obey, all that bullshit. Man and wife. *You may kiss the bride.*

Fuck you. Fuck this moment. Fuck being married to a damn psychopath.

He gives me a kiss. There isn't as much tongue as I expected, but I know I have the whole cab ride back to the hotel to deal with.

Feigning modesty, I motion towards the cab driver when he lunges at me in the cab and tries to stick his hands up my dress. I manage to keep his hands off of me, but just barely. I contemplate making myself vomit as we walk into the elevator; thinking maybe if I'm sick it will be enough of a turn off to stall him. I've never tried. I wonder how far down my throat I have to stick my finger.

The elevator doors close and he turns, closing in on me, after he pushes the button for the sixteenth floor. I look up, my heart about to implode. My breath catches in a lump in my chest, as if my lungs refuse to expand. I've never been so afraid in my life as I am in this moment. I'm only minutes away from being raped. I know better than to show my fear. I look up into his face. He hugs me and presses his lips to my neck. I feel his growing arousal rubbing me as the elevator stops and the doors open directly across from our suite.

A squeak escapes my lips. Isaiah. He's standing outside our door. Our eyes meet over Noah's shoulder and he puts a finger to his lips to hush me. He draws his gun and moves out of sight.

Oh God, he's here. He's really here. The breath that I've been holding comes out in a rush. I'm free of this madman who's rubbing my ass with both hands.

"Noah, we're here," I say, quietly.

He smiles, taking my hand and leading me out the door. He doesn't notice Isaiah standing by the wall, to the right of the elevator. He's too distracted. As he pulls the keycard out, letting go of my hand for the first time since dinner, Isaiah pulls me back. I crash into his hard chest and hot tears flow instantly at the feel of his familiar chest. He slips a phone into my hand.

"Run, baby. Just Run. Call 911." He shoves me.

Noah turns and comes face to face with the barrel of Isaiah's Glock.

I stumble, falling on these stupid stilettos. For a moment, the three of us are frozen in time. I can't run. I can't leave Isaiah behind. Knowing how crazy Noah is, I have to stay.

Now that Isaiah is here, I'm not scared.

Isaiah has his gun trained on Noah, who is staring at him with a weird smirk. "You aren't going to shoot me. You're a cop." His voice is mocking.

"Emily, I said run. Go, I can handle this." Isaiah doesn't take his eyes off Noah.

"I can't leave you here with him, he's too dangerous." My voice trembles. I glance down at the phone and remember that I'm supposed to call the police.

"911 where is your emergency"

"My name is Emily and I've been kidnapped, I'm missing. I'm..." I rattle off the details and answer questions.

As I do, Isaiah shoves Noah into the hotel room and closes the door, leaving me in the hallway alone.

ISAIAH

Not shooting this guy is getting harder by the second. I control my breathing as I follow him into the room. I pull my handcuffs out with my free hand. His black eyes watch my every move, but he isn't fighting. My heart is pounding like a drum in my chest. I can hear it in my ears as I watch him.

"She's my wife now. You can't just barge in here. She agreed to marry me," he says, finally, sitting down on the arm of a leather chair.

"She agreed because she had no choice. You kidnapped her. Man, you need some help. You don't even know her. Let's do this quietly, I don't want to hurt you." I take a step towards him. *Like hell I don't want to hurt him.*

His eyes flash with rage. "You think I don't know her? I know everything there is to know about her. Everything. I know more than you ever did. She only fucked you to get to me. She wanted me to prove myself so I did. I saved her. I showed her that she means more to me than anything. I didn't kidnap her. I brought her home." Spit flies off his lips as he yells.

"What you think isn't important anymore. You're sick. You need help and medication. Maybe you can't help it, but..."

He jumps up out of the chair. His body movement telling me that

I need to stop this conversation and get hold of this situation before something bad happens.

"Turn around and put your hands behind your back." I open the cuffs with one hand.

He laughs. "Make me."

In a flash, he reaches down and pulls a huge knife out of his dress boot. I take a deep breath, telling myself to be smart and remember my training. *Don't think about Emily. He's just another guy I'm arresting.*

"Listen to me, blondie," he starts, pacing as he points the blade in my direction, "You don't understand shit. You're just a blue-collar cop. That doesn't make you smart. You think you know things? You have no idea. She told me she loves me. She kissed me. She laid in my bed and smiled at me and told me that she wanted to marry me. It's my wedding night. She was waiting for this just like I was. You've just got her confused, that's all. She's probably scared of you. She's waiting out there for me to come and tell her that you're gone and everything is fine now. Don't get in my way."

I blink, watching him pace. His eyes growing ever more frantic as he walks, glancing around the room and watching the door.

"Did you bring that knife with you? A risk to check it in your bags, isn't it?" I nod towards the weapon.

He glances at it, the steel glints in the light as he turns it. "I'm a man of impeccable taste traveling with a beautiful woman. They would never search my bags." He laughs lightly.

I suppose that's true. "How did you know Julie?" I say, changing the subject.

My question gives him pause. He looks at me with a furrowed brow for a moment and then draws in a deep breath. "We were fuck buddies. On and off. She liked it rough." He laughs.

I don't react. All I see is her dead body lying in the front yard of her house. "She said you were her friend. Did you know she was killed?"

He nods.

I take a breath, swallowing. "Did you kill her? Was she in your way?"

He stops pacing and turns, looking me dead in the eyes. I've been holding this gun up so long it's starting to get heavy.

He doesn't speak, just stares at me. *Her throat was cut; was this the blade that sliced away her life?*

"It was that knife, wasn't it? She was your friend. I saw it on her face that she liked you when she talked about you. It must have been hard for you. I can only imagine."

"I couldn't risk losing Emily. Julie was... different. She listened to me. She was obsessed with the sex we had and I thought that it would make her... well... it doesn't matter now. Emily is mine and I did what I had to do to keep her and protect her. I love her."

"That must have been hard for you. I suppose we have to do what we have to in order to—"

He steps closer to me, and my eyes trail the knife he waves as he cuts me off. "Don't do that cop bullshit to me. The 'I know how you feel' crap that you all use to get to people. You can't get to me. You can't get inside my head."

I swallow. *Where are the damn police?* Blowing out a breath, I grasp for my next move. He's agitated. I've got to calm this guy down or I'll get stabbed or he's going to get shot. I stand in this insanely, expensive room and, for a moment, my mind is blank. I have no idea what to do or how to get this guy to put his knife down. *Could Vegas PD be any slower?*

"Noah, we are both men here. Adults. I'm sure that we can come to some agreement," I say after a moment.

"Now you want to be reasonable? Somehow, I have a hard time swallowing that. Look, I only want one thing. I've only wanted one thing all this time, and you know what that is. Bring her back in here and go away. Leave us to have our honeymoon and our lives in peace. She chose me, and you will just have to get over it." His eyes are pained for the first time since I've been in here with him.

In his head, he really loves her. I can't hold that against him. I fell in love fast too. She's amazing.

"What if I call her, and you just put your knife down so that I know she will be safe?" I suggest, with no intention of actually calling her.

"I would never hurt her." His arms fall limp at his sides.

I know it's a lie. I saw the mark on her face. He hit her. Makes me wonder what the word hurt really means to someone like him, who is clearly disturbed.

"I'd rather be safe, can't you understand that? Would you ever leave something like that to chance? Wouldn't you do everything to make sure that she is safe and protected? I love her, too."

I can see the wheels turning in his head now. He's thinking about it. Emily is his soft spot. The whole thing makes my anger sort of fade as it's replaced by pity for him. He can't help it. He's sick. Like someone with an illness who can't do a damn thing about the symptoms. That's where he is. He needs to be somewhere secure and medicated.

He needs help, not jail.

"I would, but as soon as I put this knife down you are going to arrest me. You still have the gun."

I can't give up my gun. This isn't a movie where the cop sets his gun down to get the bad guy to trust him. This is real. "I'm not allowed to give up my gun. My bosses would have my ass if I did. You understand that, right?"

He starts to pace. This could go on for hours, or even days. A standoff that ends up on the news with the hotel shut down, surrounded by swat. Emily would be somewhere out there sick with worry because I'm trapped in here with this guy.

Shit.

Maybe I should just go for it and tackle him. He's about fourteen years older, with a softer body than me, and he's a couple inches shorter. I have a shot.

But that damn knife. He could get one hand free and sink it right into me and then it'd be over.

What am I going to do?

EMILY

I press my ear to the door. My heart throbs as their voices touch my ears. *Why isn't Isaiah just arresting him?*

I lean further into the door.

"Noah, I think we can just talk like adults. You put that knife down and I'll holster my gun."

I swallow. Damn. They are both armed. Isaiah is trying to do this without hurting him. My eyes sting. This could go so badly.

Noah's words just moments ago ring in my head.

"Bring her back in here and go away. Leave us to have our honeymoon and our lives in peace. She chose me, and you will just have to get over it."

Maybe I should go in. Maybe I can calm Noah down and distract him. I wipe my sweating palms on the silk of this damn dress. *It can't be long before the police get here, can it?* It seems like it's been forever since I called them.

I can almost hear Isaiah screaming at me to get out. *But Noah... he would listen to me, wouldn't he?* He thinks I love him. I can make him see reason.

I take in a gulp of air and blow it out slowly, my hand on the knob. Carefully, I turn the knob. It's locked, of course.

I let tears fall from my tired, stinging eyes and shake my head. I can't just stand here and let something awful happen.

Here goes nothing. I rap my knuckles gently on the door. "Noah, baby, let me in." I call sweetly through tears. "Please open the door."

Holding my breath as it turns, clicks, opens. Slowly, it opens and Noah stands before me. Looking past him, the first thing I see is Isaiah, gun in hand facing the door, and me, with wide eyes that scream *what the fuck are you doing, get out of here.* I glance back at Noah, his right hand curled around the handle of that knife.

I look into the dark, demented eyes of Noah, my captor. His eyes light up at the sight of me. I walk into the room on bare feet, my shoes left in the hall. The lush carpet is soft under my feet.

"Emily... you came back." Hearing Noah say my name makes me feel ill.

I walk past him and stand between the two men. Isaiah looks at me without much reaction, but I know his eyes, and I can read them. He's upset that I came back in. I take a breath, allowing my tears to flow on purpose as I hold his copper gaze for a long moment before turning to meet this hopeful black one.

Will Noah know what I'm doing?

"Of course I came back. I'm your wife." I force the words out. They leave a sick taste in my mouth. "Why did you leave me in the hall?"

"Why are you crying, baby?" Noah asks, walking up to me. "I'm sorry. I didn't think... I just... this man..." He waves the knife at Isaiah.

"Why do you think I'm crying?" I look up into tender eyes. I hate this man so much. "I don't like the two of you in here with these weapons."

I look over at Isaiah. He lowers his gun, but holds it tightly at his side. "Emily, you...," he starts.

I glare at him. "You. You come barging in here and hold a gun on him? We broke up, remember? I'm sorry that you got hurt, but this isn't what I wanted."

"You don't have to do this." I pick up on the double meaning in his words.

I swallow and turn back to Noah. The knife is hanging at his side. "And you, letting this happen. It's our wedding day. Can't you put the knife down and let this go?" I sweeten my voice and cock my head. "Don't you want to be alone with me?"

He touches my hair. "Of course I do, but he has a gun. What am I to do, just let him take me away?"

"For what? They can't arrest you. You didn't do anything wrong. Give me this knife and I'll talk to him."

Noah furrows his brow. "I can't leave you alone with him."

My heart picks up. I need to add more fuel to the fire. "He won't hurt me. He loves me too. Please? You can wait for me in the bedroom." I take his free, empty hand and pick it up, turning it. Gently, I kiss his palm and the tips of his fingers. "Haven't you been waiting? I have." I whisper the last words.

He searches my face, and I can see that that he's holding his breath for a moment. "Of course I've been waiting for you, you know I have."

He glances over at Isaiah, who is watching us.

"Then let me get rid of him." I put his hand on my breast, knowing he can feel damn near everything through this thin fabric. "Don't you trust me?" His eyes fall to my chest. I can see that I'm getting to him. His lust and imaginary love for me seems to be more powerful than his sense of reason.

"It's not that... it's—"

I hush him with a kiss. As sick as I feel doing it in front of Isaiah, I trust he will understand. Noah dissolves immediately against my mouth. His free hand lingering on my breast; his mouth starving and invasive.

"Please," I whisper, my lips still touching his. "Let me do this. Then we can be together."

Noah takes in a breath.

"Isaiah, tell Noah you won't hurt me." I order, turning my head to meet the sick and angry eyes of the man I love.

Isaiah nods. "I won't hurt her. I love her. I just need to hear from her that she doesn't love me."

I hold out my hand for Noah. "Wait for me in the bedroom. He needs to hear it from me alone to believe it and go away. Then I will be right in. Then I will give myself to you."

Noah thumbs the blade, as if thinking about it. My heart is about to explode. *What if he realizes?* He could just stick this blade into my chest and end me right here.

Does he believe me?

The steel is cold when he lays it in my hand. I close my hand around the handle with a nod. He looks deep into my eyes and then bends, kissing me again.

"I love you so, Emily."

When I open my eyes and see the hope settling in his, I feel sad suddenly. He really does think he loves me. He's happy in this moment, thinking he's got his bride. *God, why is this breaking my heart?* He's held me captive, stalked me, and terrorized me.

Because he can't help it, that's why. He's just ill. It's not meant to be hurtful. He just can't understand.

I stand still as he walks past me, towards the bedroom. I hear the door close. As if in slow motion, Isaiah moves towards me, holstering his gun and taking the knife away from me.

"Are you fucking nuts?" he hisses in a low whisper. "You might have been killed." I meet his eyes. "But you did it. Emily…" He sighs. Instead of going on, he takes my hand and leads me into the hall where we run right into half a dozen officers.

Isaiah intercedes and explains in a rush what happened. I'm corralled and shoved against a wall by a tall woman as the rest of them disappear into the bedroom.

"Will they hurt him?" I ask. Yesterday, I wouldn't have cared. Somehow, it's different now.

"No, not if he isn't armed and doesn't fight them."

Suddenly, I hear yelling, shuffling, and a cry. Tears fill my eyes.

"No, let me go. She said I didn't do anything. She told me she loves me." His voice comes out of the open door.

It's only moments before I'm shoved away from the door and a cluster of cops comes spilling out, a screaming Noah in their midst. Cuffed and crying, his face wet with tears, he turns and sees me.

My heart breaks as I look at him. As desperately as I want to turn away, I can't force my eyes down as I start to cry myself, covering my mouth with my hands.

"Emily... Emily tell them, please. Tell them what you told me. Tell them you love me!" he yells at me.

I stand, mute.

"Why are you doing this? Didn't I do everything for you? Don't let them take me... please! Just tell them."

"I'm sorry," I call after him, finding myself wrapped in arms that can only belong to Isaiah.

I watch them drag him away; he won't walk. He's collapsed into tears, yelling my name. People are coming out of hotel rooms and taking pictures.

"Baby, it's going to be okay now," Isaiah whispers in my ear. "He will get help now."

I turn, bury my face in his chest, and sob. For myself, for Noah, and this whole thing. The man just wanted to be loved. He didn't know another way.

It's hours after statements and processing that I'm released. Treated like evidence, I feel damn near violated by the time they are finished with me. I can only imagine how much worse it would be if I'd been sexually assaulted.

Isaiah got us a room in a different hotel and stopped to buy me a few things. Now I stand under a shower as steam fills the room. Hidden behind a plastic, white curtain, as I scrub myself over and over again.

I thought I'd feel more relieved when it ended, but somehow I don't. All I can think about is the heartbreak in that poor man's face, sobbing and calling for me, as he was dragged into an elevator by four officers.

Happy to be free and with Isaiah, but sick inside over the fact that this man with all his money can't seem to find relief for his illness. I suppose that is life. He will get great doctors, be medicated, and maybe he can get some peace.

"Hey, baby?" I hear the door crack and Isaiah's voice call.

"You can come in." I sigh, I need to get out anyway. I shut off the water and he peeks at me behind the curtain. There is such relief in his eyes that it makes me smile.

"You doing okay? Can I do anything for you?"

I shake my head as he hands me a towel. "No, it's so late. You look about to collapse. I think we just need to sleep and start new tomorrow."

He leans on the wall. "He will get help now. He probably won't go to jail. You are worried about him."

I hide my face by bending to dry my hair. I don't know how to answer this, being confused by my own concern for him. Standing and flipping my hair back, I find him watching me with gentle eyes.

"You know, it's okay to feel that way. I understand your thinking, but you might want to know something." He starts, shifting as I wrap the towel around my body. He reaches for the comb on the counter he got for me and turns me to comb out my wet hair, meeting my eyes in the mirror. "I think he killed Julie."

"What? You really think that?" my voice comes out louder than I intended.

He nods, gently pulling the comb through my tangles. "Yes. His reaction when I asked him about Julie is what clenched it. I called it in while we were at the police station. The knife is in evidence and they will have it tested."

Murder. Hell. I spent all that time locked up with a killer, in his bed, in his house. I'm actually married to him until that is annulled by the judge. My blood runs cold. *Would he have killed me?* He hit me. He made vague threats with that knife when he wanted me to call Isaiah. Maybe he would have killed me.

I stare into the mirror, unseeing until he calls my name and rests his hands on my shoulders.

"Emily, you okay?"

"I have no idea."

"You're safe. Emily..." He runs a hand through his hair, releasing a sigh. "I would have hunted you down until I found you, you know that, right?"

I turn and look up into his exhausted face. Warmth floods me as I let his words sink in. He hasn't slept since I was taken, he told me so. He cried, for me. He loves me.

As I gaze up at him, I forget Noah and the echoing scene in the hallway that haunts me, the fact that I might have died, and the fear of never seeing Isaiah again. It dissipates. This man in front of me, he's mine body, heart, and soul.

"I do. I love you so much," my voice trembles.

As his arms go around me, I tilt my face up and he touches his forehead to mine. "You're my everything. I'd never let you go."

The whispered words make me hold him tighter. "Let's go to bed."

NOAH

Emily... Emily... Emily...

I struggle to call her name, but my voice isn't working. I thrash in the bed against my bonds and groan; it's the only sound I can manage.

Opening my eyes is a struggle. I see a doctor and a nurse hovering over me. One holds a needle.

"He's coming out of it."

"Looks like he's going to fight again."

The room is too bright; fluorescent lights buzz and burn my eyes as I blink, hoping that I can blink away the images of this bare room and transport myself back to my big bed where she is waiting for me.

"Mr. Burrell, do you know where you are?" the man in the white coat asks, with a heavy accent.

I blink up at him. His gray eyes accented by crows feet and smile lines. He's old. Opening my mouth, I grunt.

Why the hell can't I talk?

He looks at the nurse. "Let's give it a few more minutes to wear off. I need to talk to him. These meds they gave him were too strong." He clicks his tongue.

His hands are cold when he touches my wrist, and I jerk, but not far. Leather bands hold me into the bed. "His pulse is erratic. Mr. Burrell, you are in a safe place. Don't be afraid. You will understand soon."

Where is she? My Emily? They made her do this. Fucking cops. I spent my life taking care of cops. I built my empire around them and this is where they put me? That woman had her... she wouldn't let her come to me. I saw her crying when they took me away.

This is all just a misunderstanding. They are confused. Once they understand, they will let me go.

I feel with my thumb for my wedding band. It's gone. *Of course it is, they probably took it to fuck with me.*

They leave me for a while, laying here alone as my tongue seems to come unstuck and loosen. All I can see is her face, crying. All I can hear is her whisper, promising me that we will be together. I knew she loved me. We are meant to be together.

No one can stand between us. I proved that with Julie. I'll get out of here. I have before.

Caroline will know what to do. She did last time.

The End

AUTHORS NOTE

Mental illness is no joke, or a made up story like the one you just read. It's a very real disease that can strike anyone at any time and any age.

A little over forty-three million people are affected by mental illness in America. The National Alliance on Mental Illness (www.nami.org) stated that as many as one in five adults experiences a mental health condition every year. One in twenty-five lives with a serious illness such as the ones addressed in this fictional story. Of course, this doesn't include those that are touched by the illness. Family and friends of the affected are also touched. Those that are suffering and whose lives are touched by those that are suffering are not alone. Unfortunately, mental health is little understood and sometimes difficult to treat, but it is possible. If you or someone you know would like to learn more about how you can get involved you can visit www.nami.org for more information.

If you, or someone you know, are suffering there is help out there. Reach out to someone you know, law enforcement, or health professionals that can help you take the steps to seek assistance.

ABOUT THE AUTHOR

Rachael is a multi-award-winning author. International bestseller, and love of all things dark and twisted. Rachael lives in Houston, Texas with her husband and children.

ALSO BY RACHAEL TAMAYO

Lucifers Game

Friend Zone Series

Claim Me

Reach For Me

Chase Me

Once Upon A Kiss

Deadly Sins Series

Mine

Break My Bones

Carnal Knowledge

www.ingramcontent.com/pod-product-compliance
Lightning Source LLC
Chambersburg PA
CBHW020500310726
48979CB00016B/2741/J
9781733707398